About the author

Ever since I was little, I have always loved writing. Whether it be short stories or essays, I loved to express myself on paper. Writing, for me, is the best pastime, the best escape from reality, and I will treasure everything I have ever written.

EVANESCENT

Emily Steele

EVANESCENT

Vanguard Press

VANGUARD PAPERBACK

© Copyright 2022
Emily Steele

The right of Emily Steele to be identified as author of
this work has been asserted by her in accordance with the
Copyright, Designs and Patents Act 1988.

All Rights Reserved

No reproduction, copy or transmission of this publication
may be made without written permission.
No paragraph of this publication may be reproduced,
copied or transmitted save with the written permission of the
publisher, or in accordance with the provisions
of the Copyright Act 1956 (as amended).

Any person who commits any unauthorised act in relation to
this publication may be liable to criminal
prosecution and civil claims for damages.

A CIP catalogue record for this title is
available from the British Library.

ISBN 978 1 78465 877 9

*Vanguard Press is an imprint of
Pegasus Elliot MacKenzie Publishers Ltd.*
www.pegasuspublishers.com

First Published in 2022

**Vanguard Press
Sheraton House Castle Park
Cambridge England**

Printed & Bound in Great Britain

Dedication

I dedicate this book to Angela Thowney. None of this would be possible without her help and her belief that I could be whatever I wanted to be.

One

I can feel my stomach wrenching, as I look down at my half-packed suitcase. What am I even supposed to take with me? All I have in there so far is a pale pink pair of pyjamas, a fluffy, white dressing gown and five pairs of black ankle socks. Not that I even need those to be honest, but it made Maria get off my back about it, when she finally saw something in there. I just need to buy myself more time.

I could pretend to get the flu, or a bad sickness bug? That would rule me out for leaving surely. I mean, besides, who would let a vomiting nineteen-year-old on an aeroplane alone? You would have to be a certain type of person to do that, and Maria isn't like that surely? I know she is secretly counting down the seconds until I have to leave, and that she has already made a whole itinerary of plans for herself and Dominic for when I go, but they must still be worried about me. After all, I have stayed with them for seven years, my longest placement by far, and even they said, that they never usually keep the same foster child for longer than about six months. That must mean something!

I am due to leave for America in three days. Makes sense why everyone seems to be fussing; I guess when you think about it, that isn't long at all. I always made plans to take my education as far as I possibly could. That just because I was in care, didn't mean that I wouldn't be able to achieve the same as people with real families. And now here I am. On the verge of creating my dream life for myself, and I can't think of anything worse.

This whole thing is just really weird for me. I feel homesick almost. And I don't even think I really know what that is. Yeah, we only live in a small house, with walls thinner than paper. But these are my walls. For as long as I can fully remember. I turned into a proper woman living in this house, I started my period, dyed my hair every colour of the rainbow and slept in until two p.m. on weekends. All under this roof. Arguably the most defining moments of my life have happened here. It's quite ironic when you think about it. I hated this place when I was first sent here. I hated the way that the stairs creaked, even when I used to tiptoe. I hated the way that the heater always packed in over winter, so I would have to huddle under loads of blankets every night. I hated the fact that there were never any other kids who lived nearby to be my friends, and that the school was forty-five minutes away. I know I don't exactly have much of a life for myself here, but it's something I've learnt to appreciate over the years.

For two people who, to me, were once strangers, it's going to be so hard to say goodbye to them. And I'm really starting to doubt my mental capability.

Two

I still remember the first day I ever met them. Mrs Walters came into the room I was staying in at the crack of dawn, and said, "Pack your bags Mollie, we've found you a place, I think you'll really like this one." The six other girls in the room barely even lifted their heads. After all, this happened a lot, people being called out, and then returning to the room the exact same day, because they didn't like their new 'parents' as we would always secretly refer to them.

The care home I was in was pretty bog standard at the time, and over the years was the place I was probably in the most. The rooms were all the same, two wings, left and right, girls on the left, boys on the right. All rooms had three wooden bunk beds, and a small bathroom connected at the back. The home was purely charity supported, so there was never any electricity in the bathroom, but you kind of got used to going in the dark. Being twelve, I was never really that bothered about any of that. I remember once there was a seventeen-year-old girl in the same room as me and a few others, no one else older than fifteen except her. She had hated every second of it, demanded constant privacy, and used up all the hot water before anyone even got the chance. I felt like it brought me and the other girls closer, though. No one wanted to share a bed with her, so I would top and tail with a girl named Chloe. She wasn't with us long; she got picked almost straight away. It was a tough place to live, even at that age. Every friend you would make was temporary. You could be best friends with someone one day, and then all alone the next. Of course, I was always happy for the girls going to new families and starting a fresh life somewhere else, but it always hurt a little being left behind.

Obviously only being twelve, I barely had much to pack. I think in the end all I had was a couple of teddies, a toothbrush, hairbrush and a few items of clothing. It became impossible to keep hold of everything, especially the more places you moved. The amount you ended up losing or leaving behind wasn't even funny. I think in total, I was in six placements before this one. None of them obviously worked out, so I remember just feeling exhausted that day; I just wanted to stay in one place, moving all the time was so difficult. That's six families I was welcomed into and started a chapter of my life with, but that is also six families that I had to say goodbye to, and start all over again. At the young age of just twelve, I really just wanted to give up.

When somebody picked you, you would always go through the same process each time. The 'parents' would have four or five interviews and visits from the sisters at the home before we even found out about anything. You would then just randomly be called one morning. You would go and spend about four or five hours with the new people, in one of the recreation rooms, and see how you got on with them. At the end, you both went into different rooms, and had a chance to say whether it was somewhere you wanted to live, and for them, whether or not it's someone that they would like to take care of. I know that four or five hours isn't exactly a long period of time to get to know someone, especially a child, but you tended to be able to tell straight away if there was any chemistry.

When I first met Maria and Dominic, they looked completely different to how they do now. Maria had long, dirty blonde hair, and was wearing a grey pencil dress that went down to her knees. I remember straight away looking down at her black suede stilettos, secretly longing for the day that I'd be old enough to wear shoes like that. Dominic I just remember as seeming like a giant to me at the time. Hair gelled back neatly, with a slight amount of dark brown stubble on his cheeks, that sat just below his bright blue eyes. Maria had blue eyes too. I remember that made me feel quite special, because so did I. I remember looking at them and thinking, *maybe this is meant to be*.

They were just as lovely as you would expect someone to be in that kind of situation. She was very soft spoken, and he had a booming voice that was loud but not in a frightening kind of way. I always used to look at people, and daydream about what their lives were like. I pictured Maria as a stay at home wife, looking after children who they'd have fostered before, and Dominic going away to some office job during the day. I imagined them having a dog, running around their perfect house, and family dinners, and long movie nights with popcorn. Even the way they were dressed just seemed natural. Dominic, in a light, grey blazer with matching trousers, and a crisp white shirt. And Maria, with her black tights with a small ladder in the bottom. *I bet she was worrying about that all the way here* I remember thinking to myself.

I think for a good half hour I just sat there and stared at them, trying to pick them apart in my mind, piece by piece. They didn't try and force anything; they just embraced the silence, and greeted me back with warm smiles, and the occasional grin from Dominic. The rec room wasn't really anything special anyway, it was just a room with a few tables in, a small TV in the corner, a few bookshelves and some toys scattered along the floor. The sisters usually tried to get you to do puzzles or something with the new people as a sort of ice breaker. But this time, I didn't go for any of that. I just wanted to know more about them, and for the first time ever, I actually made the first move.

"Hi, I'm Mollie, who are you?" I remember asking quietly, as I stared across one of the circle tables at them.

"Hi, Mollie, my name is Maria, and this is my husband, Dominic. We're very excited to finally meet you." She spoke with such a soft tone, which flew out of her mouth with ease and confidence. I noticed that she had a slight smudge of red lipstick on her teeth. I liked that. It made them seem more normal to me. You would be surprised, the number of interviews I have had with people that speak like robots and look like a million dollars. I just remember these two feeling so real.

The time flew by so quickly; we just spent the whole time talking about random stuff. Even sister Mary, looked surprised I didn't reach for any puzzles or board games. I managed to find out that Dominic and Maria lived alone in a little town, that they used to have a dog called Frankie, but he had passed away a few years back, that they had previously fostered three other people, but not for very long, and that they both had part time jobs at the same bank, and planned to split the day to day tasks evenly like a team. I liked that too. Teamwork. They were both quite young, I would have guessed back then that neither of them was over about thirty. That was something that took me a little off guard when I first saw them. Typically, the people we met, who were looking to foster, tended to be a lot older, in their fifties most of the time, people whose own kids were all grown up now, so they wanted to put their empty houses to good use.

I really liked them. I felt comfortable from the very first conversation, and as soon as I was asked in the next room how I felt, I remember smiling and saying, "I'd like to go home with these people please," and to my luck, they were so delighted with how well they got on with me too, that they signed everything right away. And from there, my life really did, for the first time, change forever.

Three

I really need to start packing, I think to myself, as I am sat in the same spot on my bed, staring hopelessly at my sky-blue walls. They've been that colour since I moved here. I made the mistake back then, of wanting to impress them so much, that I just agreed to everything they asked, and when asked about the colour of the room, I told them I loved it. When truthfully, I have never been a fan of the colour blue. But even as I started to grow up, I never had the heart to tell them.

The house only has two bedrooms, and they gave me the biggest one. The other isn't much smaller, but I admired their generosity. I remember the first time walking into it; they had just had fresh, cream carpet laid on my floor, that made my feet feel all fuzzy every time I walked around. And the white furniture decorated the room comfortably. Come to think of it, I really actually haven't changed anything in this room apart from my bed. They upgraded me to a double for my fifteenth birthday, white, to match everything else of course. It's so strange now to look at it all, not so long ago, this was all brand new to me, and very soon, I will be moving to a new room far away, and for the eighth time, starting something new.

I take out everything already in the suitcase, and start again. Maria went online and ordered me a light, grey hoodie with blue writing on the front, that says 'JAYSTEAD UNIVERSITY' as a surprise, a few months back. She said it was an early going away present, but deep down, I think it was to try and get me excited for it, and mentally start to prepare myself for the new change. Seems only right that it should be the first thing I properly pack. Without even thinking, I pull out more socks to bundle with the ankle socks and place them neatly around the hoodie. I then lay my underwear next to it. Maria always said it's best to keep your smalls together, that way when you unpack, it's harder to end up losing things. Makes a lot of sense now, when I actually think about it.

What is the weather even like in Washington? I know eventually, I'll have everything with me, but I can't take it all in one go, so I need to be at least semi-prepared. I remember staying up one night with Dominic, researching the city, and all we managed to find out was that in the summer, it gets uncomfortably hot, and in the winter you'd best prepare yourself for possible snowstorms and freezing rain. Not as helpful as I had hoped.

My actual flight is on the third of October, so technically speaking, it should be quite cold. I throw a few pairs of black jeans in, and a couple of pairs of leggings just in case. We all went shopping a few weeks ago to get me some new bits for the 'new adventure' as they keep calling it. I just got a few cardigans, some pretty pyjamas and a few long-sleeved tops. After fitting all of that in, I would say I am almost halfway done.

I decide to leave it there for today. Besides, there is a lot of stuff I won't be able to pack until last minute anyway, as I will be using it right up until I leave. But I am at least content with how far I have got today. I just don't want to rush anything, at least while I still don't have to. Just getting the bare minimum done, helps me sleep a lot easier.

Four

"Welcome to your new home, Mollie," Maria said as she opened my car door for me. The journey was long but peaceful, listening to Dominic hum along to the radio, as Maria tried her best to have a go at the alphabet game.

Not bad for her first time, I obviously won though.

I stepped out onto the gravelled driveway, and took in everything that was around me. Little weeds poking in between some of the stones, the footprints you could see all over the front garden, probably from Maria and Dominic doing some gardening since it was summer. I noticed a little flowerbed right by the front door, sprouting little rosebuds and what looked like they are going to be sunflowers.

The house looked a lot smaller than I thought it would from the outside. You could tell it hadn't long been built by the cleanliness of the red bricks, and the glare from the pristine windows. I noticed an alarm system set up above the bright red front door. *Safe*, I instantly said to myself in my head. I glanced at the plaque next to the door handle, number 370, an easy enough number to remember.

As I walked into the house, I was greeted by a lovely fresh linen smell. One of my favourite smells. It was almost as if they knew. The narrow hallway was painted in a deep purple, with a silver rectangular mirror hung on the middle of the wall to compliment it. Dark wooden flooring led straight ahead of us into a closed white door. I wondered if that was the living room. Or maybe even the kitchen? I quickly slipped my black and white Converse off and put them on the pine shoe rack, like the other two had done, and passed Dominic my khaki parka coat to hang on one of the hooks mounted on the wall above. There was no way I could reach all the way up there. It even looked like Maria was struggling to hang hers, and she was still a lot taller than me.

As predicted, the door led us straight into a living/dining room. It was quite cramped, but nothing too overbearing. In one corner of the room, a grey corner sofa clung to the silver, floral wallpaper hanging on each wall. In front of it was a white square coffee table, with a few TV magazines on it. Maria probably read those at night, so her and Dominic could choose what to watch. In the other corner was a light brown dining table with four chairs, each with a grey placemat laid in front of. I loved the fact that everything was colour coordinated. It's really helping my ever-growing OCD.

The kitchen was pretty plain and simple, white cupboards, black granite worktops and white tiles. We started to walk upstairs as Maria is desperate to show me my room. Dominic grabbed my bag, and quickly follows us up. Again, upstairs the hallway was very narrow, painted the same purple as downstairs. Maria pointed to a door on our left, and said it was the bathroom. We walked a few steps forward, and we got to my room. They both stepped aside, and let me walk in.

"What do you think of the colour?" Dominic said, as his eyes fixed on mine.

"Oh, I love it, blue is my favourite colour," I said with a smile. Why did I have to say that for? But you could see they had obviously gone to a lot of effort.

"We had this carpet laid for you last week. It was wooden flooring like the rest of the house, but we thought that it might be better for you, having a soft carpet in case you want to play with some of your toys on the floor," Maria said, standing in the doorway still, looking around the room anxiously, as if to try and spot something wrong with it.

"Toys?" Dominic laughed. "She's twelve babe, I doubt she has loads of toys that she needs floor space for." Maria looked at me a little sheepishly, pulled her hands into her chest, and folded them slowly.

"No, it's perfect," I said, as I give her a reassuring smile. "I really do think I will be all right here."

Five

"You excited, Molls! Not long to go now," Dominic says gracefully, with a little too much enthusiasm for my liking. Maria is out doing some food shopping. They both joked before she left that at least they won't need to stock up the freezers with chicken and chips any more. I laughed too, but it kinda stung. The realisation now of all the little things that will be gone. I look over at Dominic, sitting on the grey sofa, in black tracksuit bottoms and a faded, blue Hollister hoodie. His style never was the best, when he was lounging around at home. But Maria loved him anyway. Whilst he just sits there sipping his coffee, one sugar and no milk (I'll always remember that) I just take it all in. The stubble that was once on his face is now replaced by an even thicker, and ever so slightly greying, beard. He said that it kept becoming too much of a chore to keep shaving every other day, so he would give a real beard a try. It took a good month or so for him to get me and Maria to stop referring to him as Chewbacca. Even the hair on his head is looking quite silver, and thinning too. I do remember him telling me that his father had a receding hairline, so he won't have that luscious hair forever. But damn, does he look old now.

It's scary. Every time I picture them in my head, it is always the same as the first time I saw them. Beautiful. And that is what they are to me. Beautiful.

"Yeah, I guess so," I say sheepishly, trying my best to sound convincing. After all, they have both saved up so much money just for me to be able to fly over there. Which they didn't have to do at all, but they wanted to, and I love them for it.

"Must be quite nerve-wracking though, I mean, I know you have moved around a lot, but this is a whole new country." Still barely taking his eyes off the TV, I know he's only trying to talk to me about it because I usually avoid the conversations completely whenever anybody brings it up.

"Yeah, I guess so, but it's a whole new chapter for me, one that I have dreamt of for years." The words fall out of my mouth quickly, and a little passively. But that is the only positive thing I have to say without lying to them. This has been my dream, and this will be a new chapter, but I just need to leave out the parts which kill me inside to even think about.

"It won't be the same without you here." He turns and faces me. "You really have changed our lives for the better. Me and Maria have been talking about starting our own family when you leave, you really brought us closer together." He looks a little uncomfortable now, his eyes still firmly on me. Dominic has never been the type of person for heart to hearts; he would even leave the room sometimes if me and Maria were getting into a deep conversation. "I have never told you this, but the reason that we went into fostering, was because I wasn't sure if I wanted to have children, and Maria, well, she's a natural, she adores them, always has done. But I didn't know if I would be able to do it. We actually ended up going on a break for three weeks not long after we got married, because we just kept arguing." His voice is starting to crack. And right in front of me, the strongest man I know is on the verge of breaking, telling me details about his past. Admitting to me the flaws they once had. The perfect couple, who have never ever shown signs of heated arguments to me or anything. I can't imagine them being so close to broken. I can almost feel tears forming in my eyes. "We decided to give fostering a go as a compromise. And we almost gave up with that as well. The three children we had before you were absolute nightmares, and we just didn't connect at all. I begged Maria to give it all up, but she persuaded me to try once more. And that was the day we met you. Standing in the doorway, blonde hair pulled back into a pony tail, black jeans, black hoodie and black shoes. The same as now really, you haven't changed much have you?" He lets out a little laugh, and looks down at the ground. "I want you to know that we will never ever forget you, Molls. I know I can give you a hard time sometimes, but I really do care about you." He reaches up and wipes a small tear from the corner of his right eye. "But enough of the soppy stuff, you're gonna be amazing and I can't wait to see the woman you're going to become."

What the hell am I supposed to say to that? I actually want the ground to swallow me up. Everything inside me hurts, aches. Who knew he had this side to him? I mean, I know he loves me and all that, but I didn't realise he thought our bond was as special as I do.

"I love you, Dom, thank you for everything," I whisper as tears fall silently down my cheeks. I step forward, and give him a hug, and just for a split second, everything stops. Everything is good again. And I don't ever want to move.

Six

I woke up a little puzzled, and it takes me a second to register where I was. No sound of five other girls snoring, no electricity generator rumbling the walls, and no constant checks from the sisters every hour, which always woke me up. I have always been a light sleeper. But this was the best night sleep I had ever had. I laid out all my teddies on my bed last night next to me, made me feel less nervous in a way.

We all sat down to dinner last night, just the three of us. It felt nice. Maria had cooked a homemade lasagne, and every time she left the room, Dominic poured salt over her plate to see how long it would take her to notice. It was so funny; I spat my drink out at one point from laughing. Maria thought it was hilarious, too, when she realised her food was now white. I liked that about them. They could have a joke together. I loved to laugh.

Again, we just engaged in some small talk after dinner. I told them about how my mother had died giving birth to me and that's all I really knew about my real family. They told me about how they didn't really have much family still around either, especially not around here, so it was just the two of them. But they both said that they wouldn't have it any other way. I wondered if when I grew up, I would be able to find a love as pure as that, I hoped so.

Next to my bed is a white dressing table with a little alarm clock on top of it, 4:14 a.m. I couldn't even remember what time we all went to sleep last night, we were all so tired, and Dominic even nodded off on the sofa at one point. Maria got some popcorn for us to throw at him until he woke up; I think it took about half the bowl before he registered what was happening.

I didn't know why I was awake this early. But like wide awake. Even at the home I never used to wake up before eight unless someone purposely woke me up. I silently lay there for a while, staring up at the ceiling, the streetlight outside my window illuminating half of my room to a deep orange. I could just about make out the silhouettes of everything in there. The wardrobe, the desk with a spinning chair, the chest of drawers and the door that led into my en suite. I think that was why they gave me this room. For my own privacy. It's a cute little bathroom with a shower, toilet and sink inside. Maria apologised last night that there wasn't a bath in there, but there was one in the other bathroom down the hall that I was welcome to use whenever I liked. I smiled and told her that I didn't think I'd ever actually had a bath before. Everywhere I had stayed previously, and the home, had always only had showers. She seemed a bit taken back by that to be honest. She promised that one night this week, she would run me the best bubble bath in the world. I was looking forward to that.

It'd been just really easy to talk to them both. Maria more so than Dominic I would say, but now I knew who to go to when I want cheering up. After about an hour here last night, I just felt normal. It didn't feel new and scary; it felt like I had been here for ages. And they both treated me straight away like I was their own. Something I had always longed for.

I felt a bit silly when Maria walked in on me arranging my teddies. I thought she would laugh at me like the other girls used to. Apparently twelve-year-olds shouldn't still carry toys with them, but I didn't have anything else. She was so lovely, and even showed me her own teddy that she had kept since she was little. She told me that she took it on holidays with her, and that if ever she felt poorly she cuddled it. She even let me have it for the night. And there I lay, cuddling Barnaby under my arms tightly, like I never wanted to let go. I wondered why she called the bear Barnaby. It was a light grey fluffy bear with a tartan scarf round its neck. Looked like the kind of bear Santa might bring you at Christmas. But either way, this bear was important to her and I was going to do my damn best to look after it, just like she had been looking after me.

I must have fallen back to sleep, as I could hear Maria and Dominic moving around downstairs. 9:55 a.m., I wouldn't have thought I would be having a lay in after my first night. I slipped out of my bed and threw on a fluffy white dressing gown Maria and Dominic had brought for me for when I arrived here. They had also given me the pyjamas I was wearing, bright yellow and long-sleeved with the cookie monster from Sesame Street's face all over. "They're so comfy," I remember saying to them last night, "I don't want to ever take them off."

I made my way downstairs, I thought they could hear me coming, as I saw Maria rushing to the bottom to greet me.

"Hello, love, how are you? Did you sleep all right last night? Do you want some breakfast?" The biggest smile is beaming off her face. She's wearing a beige, long-sleeved dress and black tights, her hair up in a ponytail just like mine, although mine was a little messy from the night before. I heard footsteps behind her.

"Jesus Christ, honey, give the girl a chance to get down the stairs before you start bombarding her with questions." He looks up at me and winked. "All right, Molls?" Funnily enough he too, is wearing beige, but in tracksuit form. Not the most flattering of colours for him to be wearing, but they looked cute all matching nonetheless.

The stairs were in an 'L' shape, and by the time I got to the bottom, I felt like I'd been doing a fashion show, with the way they were both just stood there staring at me. Maria gestured towards the front room, and I walked in confidently. The table had a whole selection of breakfast on it. My tummy was rumbling like mad. I take my seat opposite Dominic, who was already tucking into some wholegrain toast. Maria sat next to me, and said I could have anything I liked. The selection was mouth-watering. Cereals, fruit, bacon, eggs, sausages, waffles, crumpets and even bagels. All laid out neatly just for me, just in case I didn't like something they had. I appreciate the effort.

"You really didn't need to do all of this, but thank you," I said shyly as I quickly made eye contact with each of them, and then looked back down at the table.

"Don't be silly! We don't know everything about you yet, so we wanted to make sure everything is perfect!" Maria's eyes on me, full of love and hope "What would you like?"

It all looked amazing, but I thought I would stick with what I knew best. "Weetabix, please, with sugar," I said, as she immediately grabbed a bowl, and prepared it for me in seconds. It felt like that time we all had to stay in a hotel a few years back, when there was a gas leak in the care home. When you had gone so long without it, sometimes it just felt so good being looked after.

Seven

Today is the day. The dreaded day. The day my whole life changes once again. I look at my alarm clock, 3:15 a.m., not a surprise that I can't sleep. I could have sworn I heard Maria crying last night, when she went to bed. Needless to say, I cried myself to sleep too. I just feel sick. My bag is fully packed now. Maria and Dominic sat with me yesterday evening, and we just got it out of the way. At least if nothing else, I know that with their expertise, that I won't be without anything I need, when I get there.

My flight is at eleven a.m., so they will be waking up soon. Dominic said you always need to get to the airport four hours before the flight, to make sure you have enough time for everything. Not that I know what I am supposed to do when they leave me there, but with four hours, I am sure I will be able to find someone to help me. Maria said that they have set an alarm for five, ready to leave at six, which gives enough time for showers and breakfast and the traditional running around like a headless chicken, because you have lost or forgotten something. I'm gonna miss their organisation. It was a bit of a burden when I first moved here, everything is always on schedule, but I have never been late for anything since, and with my previous track record, that is definitely something to be proud of.

I must have been laying here in a trance for ages, desperately hoping that I might fall back to sleep. I doubt I will be able to sleep on the plane, so I hoped I would be at least a bit presentable by the time I arrive at campus. Apparently, my luck isn't that great this year. I hear the faint sound of an alarm ringing, and then silence. They're awake. I stand up and stretch and walk towards the bathroom to start getting ready. I always do my hair and makeup before anything else, always have done. Maria used to taunt me about it, because I would do my hair all nice, then put a jumper on and make it all messy again. She had a point, of course, but my stubbornness got the better of me, and I never managed to shake my ways.

I walk into the bathroom, and stand still for a second. Wow, this is probably the last time I will stand here. It hasn't changed one bit, since I first came here. The same white shower curtain, which is more of a cream now. Maria tried to change it a few years back, but I refused. I guess I am kind of sentimental like that. The room isn't very big at all, and you could barely fit two people inside it. The toilet is straight on the left as you walk in, opposite the porcelain sink hanging from the wall the other side. Directly next to both is a little shower room, with a drain in the middle of the floor. I never knew they existed. Apparently, they're called wet rooms and lots of people have them installed in their homes. Kinda became annoying though, at first, having a damp floor all the time after a shower, but again, something you get used to, and learn to love. The floor is totally faded now, but it used to be the prettiest lino flooring, with blackbirds all over it. They kind of just look like smudges now, but again, as I stand here and look down at it, just reminds me of my time here. This floor is worn out from me, and this shower curtain is faded because of me, and everything in this room for seven years, has been because of me. The peeling, white paint behind the toilet that I used to pick at when I spent a week in here not feeling well. The crack in the mirror above the sink, from where I opened my foundation once, and the lid flew straight into the mirror and it smashed, and the way you have to flick the light switch, three or four times for it to actually turn on. Small things for some, but for me, this is my home, and I wouldn't change it.

I hear a knocking on my bedroom door. "Mollie love, are you awake?" It's Maria, always checking on me, I'll miss that.

"Yeah, I'm awake," I shout back politely, "Just starting to get ready."

"Okay, sweet, come down when you're ready, and we can have some breakfast. Dom went out special last night, and got you some Weetabix, we know how much you love them." I can hear her footsteps going down the stairs. I don't think I have had Weetabix since that first morning here. And they remembered? And not only remembered, went out of their way with effort to go and get some for me. This just gets harder and harder.

Me and Maria picked out my plane outfit last night, nothing special, just a pair of black leggings, a white vest top, and a fluffy grey cardigan, which I have never even taken off the hanger. What better time to try it? They both said I needed something comfy to wear, apparently sometimes your legs can swell once you're in the air, so leggings will be best. I tried to act like that isn't the most traumatizing thing I've ever heard, but let's not pretend that I wasn't up worrying before bed last night, that my legs will explode, or I would die. Major hypochondriac right here. And proud. I throw on my black and white low chucks, and grab my handbag. Dom took the suitcase last night and put it in the car ready. I quickly stuff my toothbrush and hairbrush inside and close it. My hair is fine today, because Maria put it in a French plait last night, a skill I have never been able to master.

I glance at the clock, 5:40 a.m. Wow, how long was I in the bathroom for! All I did was brush my teeth, and wash my face. I'm not wearing makeup on the plane, because there's no point, and to be honest, I can't be bothered to put any on.

As I open the bedroom door, I take one last look at everything I am leaving behind, not only that, to see the room almost empty once again, is like déjà vu, one that sends chills down my spine. There's a pile of clothes on the floor near the window, stuff we went through that doesn't fit, and needs to be donated. On the very top is the fluffy white dressing gown. Funnily enough, the first thing I packed the other day. I know it's too small for me, but it was the first thing that they ever gave me as a gift when I got here. That and some awful yellow pyjamas. I guess subconsciously I wanted to hold on to it, but there was no room in the end, and Maria said she would keep it for herself as a reminder. We shared a little moment over that.

It's scary to think that looking at this now, soon it will be someone else's room, whether it be a baby that they have brought into the world together, or a new foster child. I really do pray that they can have their own family. I just hope it's not too late, Maria turned thirty-five this year, and I read somewhere that once you hit thirty, it's harder to conceive. I really want this for them, they would make great parents. I wish they were biologically mine.

To just think about the new furniture that might be in this room, the new toys to be played with, I actually wonder if Maria and Dom might move into this room when I leave? For the en suite, I reckon they would like that.

Walking down each step reminds me of the first time I climbed up them. Picture frames all over the wall filled with memories, the frames are grey just like the carpet. As I get to the bottom, I stop and stare and one of them. It's a picture of me, Dom and Maria at winter wonderland two years ago. All wearing matching grey body warmers that Dom brought, so we would be able to find each other easily, didn't do much use in the end. But that seventeen-year-old girl in the picture, smile brighter than the sun, being cuddled either side by the two most important people in her life, had no idea, that she would ever actually leave it all behind. I wish I could go back.

Eight

Maria told me last night, that her and Dominic have taken a whole week off work, just to spend with me, and help me settle in. Breakfast felt just as normal as everything else so far, definitely no complaints yet. I was back in my room now, because Maria suggested that we all go for a walk round the area, so I could see the kind of place I now lived in. Dominic seemed a little reluctant, but agreed anyway.

I didn't have a lot of clothes to my name, and it was all black, and probably too short for me. Maria promised last night that she would get me some fresh clothes to wear, pretty ones. I just took out a pair of black skinny jeans from my bag, and a slightly grey long-sleeved top that was once white. I threw on my black jumper I was wearing yesterday, gave my hair the most pathetic brush ever, but enough to make me look presentable, and headed downstairs.

To my surprise, they were both at the door ready. Maria had swapped her stilettos for a pair of suede black Chelsea boots, which went really nicely with her dress, and Dominic had on some old Nike trainers, which were on their last legs for sure. They seemed like such different people on the outside.

The walk was sweet and peaceful, the air was refreshing. It was nice to see the area. Houses the exact same as ours lined the street for miles. I wondered what families they had living inside? They told me about how Frankie would have loved this place, the fields surrounding the estate, the perfect bushes and shrubs lined up on every corner, and the number of other dogs in the area running around. I wondered what he was like. All I knew was that he was a black and white cocker spaniel, I saw him in one of their pictures hanging in the living room. A lovely picture, both of them cuddled up on the sofa with him. It was weird to think that maybe that was going to be me someday. I knew I never met him, but I reckoned I would have loved him just as much as I now love them. How strange it was, that in less than twenty-four hours, I'd found my forever family. Maybe I just attached too easily, but I couldn't think of anything worse than having to leave them. I didn't think I ever would; not by choice anyway.

Nine

I decided to skip breakfast. Dom looked a little disappointed, but I have no appetite right now, and my tummy has been doing somersaults since I got out of bed this morning. I don't like feeling trapped, and I feel like I just need to keep moving and keep my mind diverted, to soften the blow when we say goodbye. Because let's face it, it's either that or a blubbering mess over my cereal. And I could do without the humiliation to be honest, and even worse, the thought of setting either of them off is unimaginable to me.

We're all in the car now. Nothing special, just a little mustard, yellow Mini Cooper Maria took out on finance last year. Dom hates it, he says it's definitely a woman's car, but he kinda suits the image behind the wheel. Obviously, I could never say that to his face.

We don't live very far from the airport at all. I remember looking out my window for ages when I first moved in with them, you could see planes land and take off in the very distance. I used to picture what kind of people would be travelling, and where to. I spent a whole evening at my window one summer, just making up these scenarios in my head. Maria said it was sweet to have such an imagination, she was always encouraging everything I did, no matter how silly it might have been. Maybe it had something to do with there being no kids around. she wanted me to still have fun, but in my own way. After all, there's only so many board game nights you can cope with, before you need to find something new to do. Apparently, that was my fix.

I think this is the quietest car journey we have ever had together. The radio isn't even on to add background noise. The roads are empty, and the sky is a pale grey. Being October, the sun doesn't rise as early any more, and I can see the headlights reflecting off of every sign post we pass. Each one just a reminder of how far I am getting away from home. They're not even talking to each other, or holding hands like they usually do when driving. It all feels a little off to me, maybe it is just the stress of me leaving? Or tiredness? Or even Dom just wanting to drive extra carefully with the bags in the back? They're usually both so good at breaking the silence, especially Dom with his witty jokes and childish humour. Even Maria always has something to say, even at the very worst of times, she finds something. But this time, nothing. It's a little unsettling.

Funnily enough, this will be my first time abroad. Obviously, we weren't going on annual holidays with the care home, and every placement I have been in, has never really cared for them. Even Dominic and Maria haven't been further than Devon since I moved here. Apparently, airports are so much stress, and believe me when I say, how thrilled I am to be going at it alone. You would have thought I would have travelled to Washington to actually see my new home first, but Dominic set up this Skype account, and I did all my interviews and enrolment via video, saved a ton of money. I'm just praying I cope all right on the plane. My anxiety does tend to come out most in new situations, and this definitely is the toughest challenge yet.

Ten

Wow. Baths really were amazing. How had I never had one before? Whenever I saw someone having one on TV, I just assumed it was a small swimming pool or something. I didn't have the best knowledge of life at that moment for sure. But this was magical. Maria said that people had them in order to relax, and rest muscles, to which Dom chimed in, saying she wouldn't know because she couldn't lift a frying pan. Didn't really get the whole joke with that one, but I laughed anyway.

As promised, Maria went out and got me some bubbles, another new thing to me. Did you know that this was just a liquid that somehow forms bubbles, and not the type you blew yourself at birthday parties? Mind blown. They must have really thought I used to live under a rock.

The bathroom smelled amazing, Cherry Bakewell, the bubbles are called, and it smelled like a sweet shop in there; heaven. This bathroom was much nicer than my one. The whole room was a pale pink. I wonder how much persuading it took for Dom to agree to that! With matching accessories. The whole room felt so bright, even as the sun started to set, spotlights gleamed above my head, enlightening the whole room to a white glow.

The toilet and the sink next to each other on the same wall next to me, a huge person sized mirror handing right in front of the white door, and a lovely pink rug that accented the room perfectly.

I remembered Maria's top tip, never wash your hair in a bubble bath. Apparently bubbles and the liquid could make your hair go greasy faster, and the chemicals in the liquid weren't great for your hair. I must be a bit screwed now though, because my bubble beard had turned into more of a bubble hat, still looked cool though, so it was worth it.

I saw what she means about relaxation, the warm water had soothed my whole body, I felt like I could fall asleep instantly. Probably best to get out of the bath first; the last thing they both needed was to find me drowned or something.

As I stood up, the surprisingly cold air hit my body like a tornado, I was instantly freezing cold, despite it still being the height of summer. Maria had laid out some towels for me on top of the sink, pink, obviously, as everything else. I quickly grabbed it and wrapped myself up like a burrito, at that point, I just needed warmth. I looked at the water starting to fade away down the drain, and I just wanted to jump straight into it and feel the heat again.

After bracing myself for a few minutes, I grabbed my yellow pyjamas off the floor and threw them on as quickly as possible. I must have broken a timing record for that one! Despite the odd bubbles I could see in the mirror, my hair was surprisingly still dry, result. I wondered if other kids make bubble beards, if it was just a natural instinct when sitting in bubbles, to put them on your face and pretend to be Santa. I hoped so, other kids would love that. I stood there thinking for a second, how many of the girls at the home had never experienced this? How many girls were still there waiting for a home? And how did I get so lucky to be able to leave all of that behind?

Eleven

This is far worse than I could have ever imagined. Cars absolutely everywhere for what looks like miles, and people running around all over the place, dragging huge bags behind them. Dom gets my suitcase out of the car, and pushes it in my direction. I grab the handle, secretly relived to have something to steady my balance. My knees are trembling uncontrollably, and I can feel my hands going clammy. We start to walk towards a huge building, this must be it. Huge signs all around us, directing where the different terminals are, and the bag collection, not that you can see them all because of the vast amount of people weaving in and out of each other, almost in a rehearsed rhythm.

We begin to walk through a set of double doors. My whole mind has gone fuzzy, and all I can hear is the sound of Maria's heels clanking behind me, and the sound of Dom's keys jangling in his pocket. I feel so dizzy, but I need to save face. We pass an elderly couple crying as they walk past us to leave. I wonder who they have just said goodbye to? I wonder if that will be Maria and Dominic soon? And I wonder if it will be me on the other side?

This is without a doubt the scariest place I have ever been. Is it a shopping centre? Is it a food court? There's no way to tell. I have never seen this amount of people all together, since there was a fifty percent sale on at Lakeside. And this is only the first part of the airport. Judging by the size of the building from the outside, this is nothing compared to the rest.

Maria, gestures towards a sign that says departures. She says that they can't go any further past the gate, but that once I get past everything, I will have a chance to get some food and relax. Wow, this is really it. I didn't realise I would have this kind of audience when I imagined saying goodbye, but being an airport, it must just be a normal thing.

The walk feels like it's dragging madly, when I can see right in front of me that it's not actually that far. Maybe I'm just trying to drag this out a bit longer, but can you blame me? I keep turning back every couple of seconds to make sure that they are still on my trail, I must have bumped into about ten people by now, but I really don't even care. I can't be worrying about that right now.

"So this is it, Molls, you're officially a woman," Dominic jokes as he nudges me gently on the shoulder, and I tip backwards a bit too dramatically.

"I guess so," I say, not even looking at them, but at my passport, to look like I am concentrating, but really, I am just holding back the biggest lump in my throat.

"You have been a pleasure to look after," he starts. "I really mean that." He has that look in his eye again, the macho 'I'm a man so I don't cry' look, but I can see it happening.

"We love you," Maria says as she erupts into a sob and throws herself into my arms. "You have helped us both in so many ways you will never understand, I'm gonna miss seeing your little face every morning." She's hugging me so tightly that it's almost as if she has squeezed the tears out of my eyes too. So much for saving face.

"Oh, Maria, I love you both so much." I extend my arm towards Dominic to join the hug. "I wish you were my real parents, then I wouldn't have to leave." That came out all distorted, I feel like I am drowning in my own tears.

"Don't be silly, darling," Dom whispers, trying to hide the tears dripping down his nose. "We will always be your parents, not by blood, but by love." He lets out a muffled laugh as we all pull away. "You may be thousands of miles away, but you're stuck with us." He wipes a tear off of my cheek with his sleeve, Maria clinging so tightly to his other arm like her life depends on it.

I don't think there is much more to say, better yet, I don't think there is anything any of us physically can say. It's a full waterworks show over here, and it just won't stop. I grab the suitcase in my hand, and pull my handbag back on my shoulder. One more huge hug and

I just need to turn around and go. People are starting to queue around us, and I think we all need to be out of this situation. We've said our goodbyes, well, as good as it is going to get.

They both kiss me gently on the cheek and I turn my back to them and begin to move forwards. Not looking back, I just can't look back.

Twelve

The fresh smell of pancakes filled my room, like an enticing fragrance, my saliva glands watering like a faucet, and my stomach playing its own tune. I stood up slowly, and stretched until my bones cracked, no better feeling. My room was still so immaculate, I didn't dare mess it up, not after all the effort they went to, and besides, I actually wanted to stay here, I needed to act perfect.

Still wearing the same yellow pyjamas, I started to head downstairs. Maria washed them for me, when I was out in the garden with Dominic the other night; I think she realised then, that some new clothes were in order. We laid it all out and counted. To my name, I currently owned two pairs of black jeans, two long sleeve tops, three black jumpers, one coat, five pairs of white ankle socks and six pairs of underwear. Practically nothing compared to others, I usually wouldn't care, but I looked the same every single day, and when we were walking around the village, I had noticed people giving Maria and Dom odd looks, and they didn't need that.

Dom said to me in the garden that I was brave letting her wash anything of mine. Apparently, she had shrunk at least five of his suits, that year alone; but I knew she wouldn't do that to me, and even if she did, I would be fine with it, because at least she'd tried.

My feet stomped down the stairs uncontrollably. They, like the rest of the house, have hardwood flooring, except my room of course. You could always tell when someone is going up or down them, maybe that's why they had done it, so Maria could hear Dom sneaking downstairs for food at midnight? It really was an awful noise, it's extremely high pitched, and the noise rang straight through one ear to another, and this was on every single step. I wondered how they had coped with it? Then again, it must just have been something that they had gotten used to.

Like always, I saw them both appear at the bottom to greet me. I mean, it was hardly like they didn't hear me, an elephant in a circus made less noise than these steps, and don't get me wrong, I knew I may be a little bit chunkier than your normal twelve-year-old, but I wasn't that heavy surely?

"You all right love? I'm gonna take you out shopping after breakfast if that's okay with you? A nice girls' day out, what do you think?" Maria was standing there, giving me the most, hopeful smile I had ever seen in my life, bless her.

"I would love to, that would be great!" I said as I jumped down the last few steps, the noise not much louder compared to walking.

"Jesus Christ Maria," Dom sniggered. "Is it a new tradition now to host an episode of question time and interrogation as soon as you hear her move?" Maria just rolled her eyes and in we walked to the lounge.

Sitting in front of where I usually sat, is a stack of pancakes bigger than my head. I could see droplets of syrup smothering them as I got closer. I thought I was in love. Maria asked me the night before if I liked pancakes, apparently Dom liked to make them from scratch. 'I can't wait to try them,' I remember saying as we all went to bed last night, and they truly lived up to my expectations. Every mouthful burst with flavour, I was in complete heaven, the pancakes, so soft, and felt almost tender as they danced around my mouth perfectly. I couldn't stop eating them, I took mouthful after mouthful until the plate was pretty much cleared; I wished I had one more to mop up the syrup with.

Despite me having almost double the amount of pancakes compared to them two, we finished eating at the same time, I will never forget the smug look on Dom's face with pride, when he saw my empty plate. He even teased that he might make them every morning so he would be my favourite. It was like they were having a bit of friendly competition, but regardless, I still loved them both.

It's only about quarter to eight, by the time I reached the top of the stairs. We probably wouldn't be awake at this time normally, but Dom went back to work for his first shift that day, so they needed to be early risers. Not that I minded, I mean, being woken up to that smell was fine with me. I passed their bedroom on the right, directly opposite the big bathroom, I took a peek in as I did every morning, bed made perfectly, fresh flowers on the windowsill, giving the room more flair, and not one thing out of place. The room unsurprisingly was grey, the same as downstairs; they must have been huge fans of the colour. The wooden flooring flowed into it beautifully, and the double-glazed windows sat comfortably, above the crushed velvet headboard. I loved this room, the built-in wardrobes, the huge telly hanging off the wall, the little decorations dotted around to make it look less plain, everything was so enticing to look at. Maybe when I was older, my room would look like this?

Back in my room now, it was nice having everything washed, because now I didn't have to worry so much about accidentally spilling something on myself, because I knew I had clean clothes as a backup. I stepped into my black jeans, and pulled my t-shirt over my head gracefully. it still fitted the same, I was very thankful for Maria. I vigorously brushed the knots out of my hair, and put it up into a little bun, knowing full well that putting it up was what causes me to have knots, but I preferred it being out of my face, just not enough to cut it short.

Dom was dropping us off into town on his way to work. They only have one car so we would have to get the bus back, but that should be fun. This was the first time I had been back in this car since they'd brought me here; it was some kind of Toyota I think, one of those cars that you'd have to climb behind the passenger seat to get to the back. It was bright red though, which I loved, because that was my favourite colour.

Dom looked so smart in his work suit, even more so than the day we first met, he was wearing a blue tie for starters, which matched his blazer and trousers fittingly, topped off with a pair of black, shiny suit shoes similar to the ones he'd worn before, and of course, that crisp white shirt. It looked really expensive; no wonder he got funny with Maria washing his clothes.

Town really wasn't far at all, fifteen minutes if that. He pulled over outside a main entrance labelled 'CRIMSON MALL' and me and Maria quickly hopped out. There must have been over five hundred cars there. We'd only stopped for a second, and it already looked like a pile up. I thought that must be the quickest I had ever said the word 'goodbye' to someone before, but I was still happy, I was with Maria, a girls' day sounded lovely.

This mall had three floors, just full of shops. Every shop you could ever think of, all lined up solidly, for as far as my eyes could see. I reckoned that this was what people experience when they go to Disneyland, I was in utter awe. The pretty lights hung elegantly above us, the gorgeous topiary dotted around the centre with white, wooden benches, full of people eating and talking. I stopped for a second, as Maria grabbed a map, just to take it all in, so many different people all in this one place, I had never been anywhere like this in my life, I mean, I had been shopping, but only to little outlet stores or supermarkets, and this place had absolutely everything.

"So, Molls, where do you want to go first?" Maria said whilst carefully eyeing up the map, which has now unfolded into at least A3 size.

"I don't know, I have never heard of any of these shops, where would you like to go," I said as I looked up and down and all around me, eyes wide, and mouth open like I was in shock.

"What about Claire's, it's just up here to our left, we could get you something pretty for your hair." Maria pointed to her left, and I saw a grey and purple sign. She had been saying for a couple of days now, that she was so jealous of my thick hair, and that she wanted to experiment with it, whatever that meant.

"Yeah, OK, I would like that," I said as I started to walk, we passed three shops, Apple, Sketchers and EE, Claire's was a good choice I reckoned, as these ones all looked a bit technical to me, and from what I could make out, sketchers sell chunky footwear that older people wear to help them walk, yep, definitely didn't need any of those just yet.

This shop definitely looks bigger on the outside than it is on the inside, maybe that's just because there was so much there. Everything a twelve-year-old could ever need, keyrings, fluffy notebooks, headbands, handbags, stationary, teddies the lot, and that isn't even half of it.

To our luck, there were only about three other people currently in there, so that way we didn't feel rushed. I walked straight over to the keyrings, one instantly caught my eye, it was a purple dolphin that was flocked and had speckles of glitter around it. This may actually be the cutest thing I had ever seen. It was weird, I must be surrounded by at least one hundred keyrings, all hung on little hooks all the way up the wall, all different sizes, shapes and colours, and I go to this one, arguably one of the smallest in there. I just love it.

"Oh wow, what have you got there, love?" Maria said softly, as she appeared behind me with a few things in her hands.

"It's a little dolphin! It's so cute, and it even feels fluffy," I said forcing the keyring at her to feel what I felt.

"Oh bless! That is very cute! You can have it if you want?" Her smile beaming, almost lighting up the room.

"Yes, please," I said so quickly, it almost came out like a shout. "Look there's a yellow one here too," I said as I took the dolphin off the hook. "You should get it, Maria! Then we can be matching!" I was full on excitedly shouting by this point. Jumping up and down almost, how perfect would it be to have something like that together!

"That's a lovely idea! I would love to have something matching with you!" She picked it up and stared at it for a few seconds "I will put it on my keys, that way I will always be reminded of you when I am out." I was so happy, this was so exciting! I had never had anything like this before. I remembered at the care home, some of the girls had friendship bracelets, and this was like our own version, the foster mother and daughter adaptation.

"Look, I found these over there," she said as she handed me a black suede Alice band and a pack of black scrunchies. "I chose black to match everything you already have at home, but they have loads of other colours if you would prefer something a little different."

I really like them, I didn't know if it was just because I had always worn black, but everything in black just automatically looked better to me.

"These are perfect!" I said giving her my biggest smile.

"I thought an Alice band would be ideal for you, so we can have your hair down sometimes, but it will be out of your face, and scrunchies are always my favourite thing to wear in my hair when I have it up, they will look so pretty on you." The fact that Maria had thought this all through was wonderful, stuff I wouldn't have even thought about, especially with the Alice band, and the fact that she wanted me to have scrunchies like she does was making me feel so warm inside, not only that, but the fact that she chose black as well, shows that she really had been paying attention to me. I had never really had that from somebody before.

Maria paid and we left the shop gracefully. I told her I would carry the little purple bag as it was stuff for me inside. I must have thanked her about a million times whilst we were standing at the till. I'm not used to people spending money on me. Everywhere else I had been had just been like essentials, new shoes if current ones break, hand me down clothes from the other girls, and elastic bands from the office at the home for hairbands. Obviously never being in my placements long, I was never really treated to anything. Which was fine, I wasn't complaining, some people didn't get the chance for a placement, but being treated how I had just been in one shop made me feel so special, all over a keyring, an Alice band and some scrunchies? I couldn't stop smiling either, and this was just the start to the day.

As we started to head further into the mall, I walked closer and closer to Maria, I just didn't want to lose her, not in here of all places. She was walking so confidently, checking every couple of seconds that I was right beside her. Her grey, knee high boots clanking on the tiles as she took each step, they went really nicely with her white jeans, and a denim jacket to match. I envied her style, but I knew I could never pull anything like that off.

The next shop we found ourselves in is Converse. Wow, who knew they had their own stores dedicated to just that one brand. I had always worn Converse for as long as I could remember, no one ever really cared about the price of them, because they lasted really long so it was always worth it. Having said that, they were always hand me downs, or charity shop bought, still worked for me though, so that's all that matters. I had learnt over the years that it didn't have to be new, it just needed to be something, and as long as it fit, it was perfect for me.

This shop really was something though. Who knew there even were this many colours for shoes, reds, greens, yellows, oranges, pinks, the list went on and on. Trainers stacked to the top of every wall, high tops, low tops, knee high, so many different styles, I was in shoe paradise. We walked over to the junior section at the back of the store, you wouldn't believe the sizes of some of these! How could feet be that small?

"Pick any pair you like, darling," Maria said as she took a seat on a stool directly in front of them. Wow, what a decision to make, should I get new black ones like I was wearing, or should I get a new colour altogether? I was thinking about what Maria would want me to get, what her vision was for me to look like. I thought she would have chosen these white ones, unlike the ones I was wearing now, these were low compared to high tops. I picked up the shoe and examine it carefully, not that I was looking for anything in particular, but to look like I was really involved in the choosing of them, I could feel Maria's eyes on me anyway, so I wanted to look like I really cared about everything.

"I really like these ones," I said as I turned and faced her to show her the shoe in my hand. "I have never owned a pair of white shoes before, and I saw that Dom has some like this, so they must be comfy."

Maria smiled and let out a little giggle. "I think it's a great idea, I was secretly worried you would go for the plain black again, and the ones you have on now, we can use as a backup pair, what do you think?"

"That's such a good idea! I could wear these ones when I am going out and it's raining, or helping you in the garden, and these white ones when we go out somewhere nice together." I could feel myself start to fill with excitement again, I thought it was just the idea of imagining a proper future with them, I felt like I was already starting to build my life.

We left that shop with another bag for me. I felt so grateful and just full of love. It was also such a nice surprise, to find out that me and Maria had the same shoe size! Four and a half exactly, these things couldn't just be coincidences for sure! But at least I knew that when I was old enough to walk properly in them, we could share high heels!

The rest of the shopping trip went pretty smoothly. I managed to get a pair of white and a pair of blue skinny jeans, to go nice with my new shoes, a new pair of pyjamas with puppies on, some more socks and underwear, and a few tops.

To our delight it was actually so close to the time Dom finished work — who knew we had been here for so many hours — but it was so nice being able to take our time and have fun, I think I laughed more that day than I had in ages.

Dom texted Maria, suggesting that we eat out that night. The fact that this place was full of restaurants, seemed like a good idea, that and the fact that mine and Maria's stomachs had been rumbling for a good hour or so. We did stop for lunch after we left the Converse shop, we just popped into a place called Greggs, and had a sausage roll each. That was life changing, by the way.

Not long after the text, we met Dom in the car park to get rid of these bags in the boot. I had played it cool all day, but any longer, my arm would fall off. Walking back into the mall, Maria handed me the map from earlier, and there was a list of all the food places on there, and they told me to pick whichever one I thought sounded best. It was a very tempting list, how could I choose out of these:

- TGI FRIDAYS
- WAGAMAMA
- WILDWOOD
- PIZZA EXPRESS
- MCDONALD'S
- KFC
- BURGER KING
- BILL'S
- PIZZA HUT
- SUBWAY
- GREGG'S

- CAFÉ UNO
- DEAN'S DINER
- WIMPY
- NANDO'S

I decide to rule out Gregg's, Subway, McDonald's, KFC, Burger King, Café Uno and Wimpy. This was either because I had been to them before, or because they didn't serve appropriate meals for a sit-down dinner. I didn't really fancy pizza either because we had that last night, I wanted to think about them as well, and what I thought they would like.

After realising that I had been stood here staring at it for about five minutes, I chose Nando's, no particular reason really, but I remembered at the home people would boast about being taken there for food, and I always felt slightly jealous. All I knew was that it was a chicken restaurant, and who didn't like chicken? So I figured it would be a pretty safe bet with Maria and Dom.

"Good choice!" Dom shouted. "We love a cheeky Nando's, don't we?" he nudged Maria on the shoulder playfully.

"We certainly do! Let's go and get a table before we all starve to death," Maria said as she started walking. Luckily, Nando's wasn't very far from the entrance, my feet felt just about ready to fall off, I didn't know how Maria had coped in those boots.

The meal was absolutely delicious. We all had exactly the same, butterfly chicken with two sides. I chose mash and garlic bread, the others chose chips and rice. They also did this thing called a bottomless drink! What an idea! I must have had about six glasses of Fanta before the food even came out! After all, it was my treat day, and I would just make sure I brushed my teeth extra thoroughly tonight.

What a wonderful day, I thought, as I put on my brand-new pyjamas. They were blue that pretty much matched the walls, and I believed the puppy on them was some kind of golden retriever. It felt a little weird not wearing the cookie monster ones, but these ones had a new sentimental value to me, my first proper day out here. I grabbed my new keyring out of the bag on my floor, and climbed into bed. I would always keep this with me, always. As long as I had this, I had them, and I was safe, and I hoped Maria keeps hers forever.

Thirteen

As I take each step forward, everything just becomes blurrier and blurrier. My tears forming quicker than a lightning bolt, and my hands tremble to the sound of my heart beating. People pushing past me at every angle, security lined up against every wall, armed with guns, as we pass through the metal detectors. One guy, in the one next to me, got stopped, and instantly searched, he was then walked into a side room. Damn, I wonder what they found?

I really don't want to put my suitcase on the conveyor belt, I need it with me, I need to know that everything inside is safe, I can't even risk losing anything that they brought for me, let alone something I desperately need when I get there. Dom said that there will be about four hundred other people on the same flight with me, how is that even possible? As I stand here staring down at my black suitcase, I think to myself, how can you even fit four hundred of these on board, let alone actual people? My head starts to feel fuzzy, and I feel faint. Everything I have tried my best to avoid thinking about, in regards to the flight, is all crashing round my mind like a carousel with no stop button. It really just doesn't seem possible to me that something can hold all that weight, whilst still being able to stay in the air for eight hours. Oh my god, eight hours. I can't do this.

"Excuse me, miss, are you okay?" A man appears from behind me, wearing a thick, black jacket, with 'AIRPORT STAFF' written on the left-hand side. He must be boiling wearing that! I mean, I know its October, but I feel like an actual radiator at the moment, probably the stress of crying though to be honest.

"Erm... yeah... sorry," I say nervously, trying to hold back more tears. "Erm, I just have never been to an airport before, so I'm not really sure how to go about things."

"Ah, I see, well, don't worry, we just need to get your suitcase on here with the others," he says as he begins to take it from my hands. "That way we can make sure that your bag gets delivered safe and sound with you at the other end." He keeps staring at me and letting out what can only be described as a reassuring smile. He actually looks fairly young, twenty-seven to twenty-eight I would guess, hair in a ginger quiff, no facial hair, and a slight glimpse of a tattoo on his neck.

"Okay, and then when I get to Washington, it will look the same the other side, right? Just take it off a conveyor belt like this one." He must think I am a proper idiot.

"You really weren't joking when you said you have never been to one of these before, were you?" he says politely as he smirks and carefully places my case on the belt with the others, and within seconds, I can't see it any more. "For the most part, yes, all airports have the same system. The other side will look different of course, but for all intents and purposes, we all seem to operate the same. You have already done the hard part; security. You would be surprised the amount of time people get held up there for earrings, or metal buttons on clothing." I start to feel less nervous. Instead all I can think about, is a bunch of people being scolded for wearing the wrong clothes, maybe that's what Dom meant, when he said you need to allow yourself a lot of time. "From here, you just walk up towards that revolving door over there, there will be signs directing you either left or right for where you are headed. Walk the right way and you will come to the final port before boarding, there you can have a drink or a bite to eat, and also have chance to relax." His tone is almost mesmerising, I am taking in every single word he says to me, and understanding it all completely. I don't feel scared any more, I just feel like I now know where I need to go, and how to get there, and it is taking a lot of the edge off.

"Thank you so much!" I say wiping a speck of sweat from my forehead. "You're a life saver." I take a look at his name badge at the top of his jacket, 'Felix' what an unusual name! But I kinda like it.

"No worries, ma'am, you enjoy your flight, and we hope to see you again soon." He is gone before I even get the chance to reply, off helping someone else, hopefully just as lost as I felt five minutes ago. It's funny he said that, I hope to see myself here again soon as well. Back to the place where my life feels whole.

He wasn't kidding about those signs. As soon as I pass through the door I see a huge illuminated sign to my left saying 'WASHINGTON DC' and one to my right saying 'LAS VEGAS (NEVADA)'. It's actually quite funny standing here for a second, watching the kind of people going each way. Left, is full of people in business suits carrying briefcases, and right, filled with big groups of people, ultimately going to gamble their lives away, and then there's me, somewhere in between both I guess.

The departure lounge is surprisingly nice, pristine white walls, tiles have turned into thin black carpet, and grey leather chairs all over the room in neat lines. To my immediate left is a vending machine full of crisps and chocolate, and what appears to be some kind of drink dispenser next to it. I am starting to think maybe I should have had those Weetabix after all.

The atmosphere in here is very calm; the boarding door straight ahead, bolted shut with stanchions in front of it. I take a seat to my right, opposite the machines. There aren't too many people in here to be honest, and they all seem to be keeping to themselves which is good. Maria said that there's usually lots of different lounges for one flight, mainly for people travelling at a higher class, so hopefully it won't get too cramped.

Luckily enough, I still have some loose change at the bottom of my handbag, three pounds fifty to be exact. Everything else is in the suitcase, and we switched all the money in my purse last night to dollars. I should have a Uber or something waiting for me when I get there, to take me to campus, but apparently you should always be prepared, just in case you have to take matters into your own hands.

More people are starting to flow into the lounge, so I decide it's better now than never to get some snacks, overpriced as always. I punch in the numbers and manage to get a packet of Ready Salted Walkers, a Twix, and a packet of Fruit Pastels. All come to three pounds forty, and of course, the machine doesn't give change, so that's ten pence I will never get back.

I guess thinking of it, I don't really need any of this, there is a meal on the plane, some kind of pasta dish I ended up choosing in the end. It's going to be microwaved regardless, and you can't really go wrong with pasta. But for some reason, I just had a little panic sitting in that chair, maybe it's because everyone around me seems to have something with them to eat, and what if I don't like the plane food? I have already gone without breakfast! I shove them in the bottom of my bag and retake my seat in the same place. It seems like people are trying to sit as close to the door as possible, not really sure why though, the seats are allocated anyway, so the quicker that you get on, the longer you have to wait for everyone else to find their seats.

"Can everyone begin to grab their hand luggage and start to form a queue, we will be boarding in approximately ten minutes," a very smartly dressed woman confidently bellows at us from the other side of the room. As she says that two more women walk over to the door in preparation to check people's passports and stuff. They are all wearing red waistcoats, white collarless shirts and black trousers; they also all have a red ribbon tied up in their hair, and black matching kitten heels. I wonder if they are forced to wear those shoes? I wouldn't want to be standing still all day in those, for sure.

As instructed, everyone moves quickly towards the door, forming a line in an orderly fashion. There must be about one hundred people in front of me and around two hundred behind. I wonder how many times these people have been on a flight to Washington, or to anywhere for that matter. I take a quick look around at all their faces, no one even looks phased in the slightest to be boarding a plane, I must just be the only one, then.

The line moves very quickly. Like I saw with the others, I have my passport and my boarding pass in my hand ready. With it now being my turn, I hand my documents over to one of the women. Sandra her name is. Her hair is the same shade of blonde as mine, small world. She tells me to have a good flight and before I know it I am in seat 212C, sitting at the window, next to a brown haired businesswoman, slim build with olive coloured skin. I'm glad it's a woman and not a man, not that I have anything against men, but I reckon I would feel slightly uncomfortable, especially every time I got up to go to the toilet.

One of the stewardesses begins to give the health and safety speech, not that I can actually see her with all the rows of people in front of me, but I try my best to listen anyway. I attach my seatbelt with everyone else, and we start to move.

As I take one last look out the window, as England fades, smaller and smaller into the distance, I can feel a little tug at my heart. Maria and Dom are down there, and for all I know, I might not get to see them again.

I feel really tired. I think not sleeping worked in my favour, because I can feel my eyelids beginning to droop. If I can manage to sleep on this flight to pass some time, then it will be so worth it. I need to focus on blank thoughts, not what I have left behind, or what I am throwing myself into, pointless things that make no sense; it has to be my only distraction.

Fourteen

It's Saturday now, and marks two weeks since I arrived. I couldn't even begin to express how normal everything was for me, without even realising it; we had all adapted a little routine. I wondered if they felt as complete having me in their lives, as I did having them in mine. Having said that, I did get completely freaked out the other night by the stairs. I had got up to get some water, and the noise scared me so much, to the point I just sat down and cried. It's normal for everyday sounds to be scary in the dark, right? Anyway, I ended up sleeping in their bed with Maria that night. Dom took up my room as a compromise, and I fell straight to sleep. It was really nice knowing I had them both there when I needed them. I didn't even want to go into how utterly humiliated I was for them to have seen me cry, so much for saving face. But no one had mentioned it since, and they both made sure I had a drink with me every night, just to avoid any recurrences happening again.

Neither of them had work at the weekends, so that day was our first, out of two, lie ins. You can tell it was their favourite part of the week, and mine to be fair, sometimes you just needed to relax.

It was quarter to eleven, and I could tell I was the only one up. They had had such a busy week, so I was glad they were still resting, mind you, I had no idea how Maria managed to get any sleep with Dom's snoring, it woke me up some nights.

I switched on my little TV, sitting on top of the chest of drawers, quietly of course. I had never actually watched anything on it yet, and Maria had brought some Disney DVDS for me the other week, just in case I ever wanted to be on my own, she was so thoughtful like that. After a few seconds contemplating, I chose Aladdin, one of my all-time favourites. Disney movies were all we ever really watched at the home. I reckon Maria chose them to try and make me feel more settled.

I snuggled up back in bed under my duvet, my teddies still surrounding me, just where I'd left them. I grabbed the remote, and put on subtitles for the film, and turned it down even quieter, although it was only a small screen, my eyesight was pretty good, and this way, no one got disturbed.

I could probably recite this word for word if I tried. My favourite character was Abu, I just thought he was so cute, and I loved that he was always there for Aladdin, and the fact that they were best friends, because it didn't always just have to be blood family that you connected with, like me Maria and Dominic. I would do anything for them, and I was sure they would do the same for me.

"Hiya love, you all right?" I must have been about half way through the movie by now. Maria was standing in my doorway, still in her pink, silk pyjamas with her name sewn into the left breast pocket.

"Morning," I said cheerfully, as I began to sit up. "Did I wake you?"

"Oh no! Not at all! I just came to check on you, what are you watching? Aladdin? My favourite." Of course it was her favourite! We were practically the same!

"Yeah! It's my favourite too! Do you wanna watch it with me?" I mirrored her sweet smile, as I gestured with my arms for her to come in. She looks a little stunned, but in a good, unexpected way.

"I would love to!" I moved to closer to the wall, and Maria got into bed next to me, and there we were, both lying in bed, watching a cartoon on a Saturday morning. Bliss.

The end credits started to roll, and I grab the remote and switch off the TV, it was quite nice just sitting there in silence actually, the company was wholesome, and I had always longed for someone to be around, where without even talking, you enjoyed each other's presence. It was a very warm feeling.

"Now that we are coming into the middle of September, I was thinking maybe we could talk about schools?" Maria said openly, as she turned to face me.

"Oh, okay," I said, a little hesitantly, I hadn't even thought about schools once, since being there.

"I know you said that you were previously in a primary school on and off. Tell me about it, I would love to hear more." Bless her, she always tried so hard to find out about me, not in a patronising way, in a way that showed that she cared, and was truly interested.

"I went to a school called Cresthall. I didn't finish most of the years though, because I was moving around, but it was nice that every time I did have to go, it was the same place that I knew." I kept looking down at my hands, I didn't know why, but it always felt like such a tricky subject trying to explain the past, not because it was particularly bad, but because it unfolded a whole lot of past memories, past families, and past moments that I could do without remembering. "I was just lucky that the families that took me in, lived quite local to it. It wasn't a very big school, probably around two hundred pupils altogether, but it was somewhere safe for me, like it didn't matter me moving house, because I still had that one place that was familiar to me. I know I didn't say before, but it was the only thing making me a tiny bit scared about moving here, when I found out how far away, I now live." I glanced up, and she was staring straight into my eyes, projecting empathy from her very core. I felt comfortable sharing this with her. "There was this one girl called Holly, who, even after I kept leaving and coming back, would always play with me. She was my only friend at the time really, and I was fortunate to always be put back into her class every time I returned. She was really nice, she had the longest ginger hair you could ever imagine, with freckles all over her nose, people picked on her for it from time to time, but I never understood why, like she can't change them, and I always thought she looked fine." The words were just flowing out of my mouth so easily. This felt like a proper little conversation, and Maria was showing so much interest, I didn't want it to end. "My favourite subject was literacy. I struggled with the rest, especially maths, as I ended up missing so many lessons explaining how to do things, but with literacy, I could just go into my imagination and write about stuff that I wanted to write about. My spelling wasn't great, but it was readable, so that's all that matters really." I smiled, and Maria let out a little titter, reminding me once again, how alike we must be, I wondered if she is feeling it too? Her silence just gave me more ammunition to keep talking. It was nice, feeling valued. "There was this huge field in the playground, that in the summer was the best place to be, we would build birds' nests out of the piles of cut grass, and practice our dances that we would learn in assembly. I loved assemblies too, we would have one every morning without fail, and sing hymns to each other. It was a different experience for sure, but even now, it is something I wish I still had going on in my life, it was a nice time for everyone to act as one, you didn't care who you were next to or who you were, because we were just all there, exactly the same, singing the exact same songs, not having to hide away, I liked that." She must have thought I was just rambling on now for sure, but nothing about her body language would suggest anything of the sort.

"How lovely, we used to sing songs when I was younger in school as well, and don't worry so much." She let out a laugh, "I was awful at maths, I still am, don't tell anyone though, the bank would have me fired." I laughed with her at that, I mean, if someone who was bad at maths, could successfully work in a bank and do well, then there was hope for anyone with what they aspired to do. You just needed to have the confidence for people to have faith in you. "Holly sounds great. It's a shame as you say about the bullying, kids can be so awful these days, and I completely agree with you on the not thinking anything of it, it's what's on the inside that counts, always remember that." She reached up her arm, and cupped my face in her hand for a few seconds. She felt warm and comforting.

"Of course," I said, giving her a wide smile. "Are there any schools around here?" I asked quietly.

"There is one high school, Pilters Academy, it is about forty-five minutes away, and funnily enough, is the same secondary school Dom went to when he was your age." Wow, how perfect was that! "I know that obviously the school year has technically already started, but we were thinking maybe it would be an idea to see if you wanted to try it out?" Every time she spoke, her words felt so sincere and honest, I felt like she could convince me into anything without even trying.

"That could be fun," I said, looking down again, but not so obviously. "I have never been to a big school like that before."

"I promise you now, they are not as scary as you probably think. I know of course at the home you had more of a home-schooling routine, but we thought you might like to go and interact with other people, gain some life skills, and go on some amazing trips. Please don't take this the wrong way, though, we are in no way forcing you and if you decide against school, we can work around that. We just want to support you, and obviously, if school is something you have been thinking about, we don't want to hold you back. You have been here a little while now, and settling in so well."

She was completely right, I had been there for a few weeks, how time flies! All of this though just seemed like a good idea to me, because if I went to school here, then hopefully I wouldn't have to leave them or move somewhere else, and if they were thinking about it too then they must have really loved having me there.

High school had always been something I had avoided thinking about. I mean, in movies, it's always big schools where kids got bullied and hurt, and as you got older, the more you evolved into an adult, and that thought alone made me weak at my knees.

I just really didn't know if I was ready for it. It would have been different for sure, if I had completed all of primary school, but I would be with people so far more advanced than me, and going somewhere new was tricky enough, let alone not knowing anything the kids would have been taught previously, it was just a little daunting.

But again, I knew it was what Maria and Dom would want for me, and I wanted to show them that I could try new things and that I was mature. Maria said to let her know once I had had a proper think about it, but I just didn't know, I really didn't know.

Fifteen

"Excuse me, sorry," I can hear faintly, as my tired eyes struggle to open "Would it be possible to pull the cover down on your window, it's really glaring off my TV screen." How long have I even been asleep for? I can't remember anything.

"Yeah of course! Sorry," I say immediately shooting up and closing it, I'm not bothered that she woke me for it, it's a long flight, and there's nothing worse than not being able to watch something properly.

"Thank you, sorry to wake you up," she says innocently.

"No, it's fine, sorry, I should have closed it when we took off, would have saved you getting half way through a film, not knowing what's going on." I smiled at her "How long have we even been in the air for?" I feel like the more and more I try to sound like I am not completely new to this, the more obvious my questions become.

"About three hours now, our food should be coming shortly, I thought I would wake you now, so you can at least prepare yourself a bit first." She laughs, and all that does is worry me about the food. I am absolutely starving though, I grab my bag and take out the fruit pastels, probably the best thing for me, the sugar will give me that energy I'll need.

"Would you like one?" I say as I offer the packet to her before I start eating them. She nods her head to decline, but with an appreciative look on her face.

"No, thank you, I don't really eat sweets, doesn't stop me buying them for my kids all the time though!" We share a small laugh, small but real.

"Oh, you have children, how lovely, how old are they?" I say, trying to make conversation, mainly, because I have been pressing play on my TV screen for about five minutes now, and it's not doing anything.

"I have two, I have a seven-year-old boy called Colin, and a one-year-old girl called Naomi, and my name is Harriet by the way." She extends her arm and we shake hands, gracefully.

"I'm Mollie, it's nice to meet you, and how sweet! I always said that if I ever had children, I would want one of each!"

"They are the best, definitely a handful, but my ex-husband splits custody so it means I can still travel for work all the time." She speaks a little off-tone, but still answers, and gives me more of an insight without even having to ask.

"That's good then," I say, trying not to sound like I am prying. "What do you do?"

"I work as an accountant, that's what I travel to DC for, three days a week. I have the children the other days back in London." Still not even bothered about anything that she is saying, like it is completely normal.

"Oh wow, what a huge amount of travelling, and here I am, on my first ever flight on my way to a new university." I have on my 'interested' voice now, not that I'm not, but I have a habit of zoning out in conversations, and I don't want her to think I am being rude.

"Oh, how boring, what do you even say to someone as foolish as that? Good luck, I suppose," she says as she puts on her headphones and resumes her film. I guess some people just aren't that interested when they aren't talking about themselves.

I finally manage to get a film to work, after about another fifteen minutes of frustratingly tapping at the screen, Harriet however, kept looking at me in disgust almost, like thanks for the help.

I choose *The Incredibles 2*, I haven't seen it before, which sucks, because when they first announced they were making a sequel a few years back, me and Dom promised we would go and see it together. To be honest, there aren't really many movies on here I do want to watch, and I have pretty high hopes for this one. Maybe if it is that good, I'll watch it a second time afterwards.

I actually feel instantly better after the Fruit Pastels. I knew I just needed a sugar kick. I'm glad Harriet didn't want one now, each one tastes like heaven in my mouth, but I am still anticipating the pasta on its way. Even if it is horrible, it will still stop my stomach grumbling like a walrus.

"Hi, I'm Sophie. I have a tomato and basil pasta bake with Mozzarella cheese for a Mollie Fitzgerald, and a beef wellington for a Harriet Walters." She looks exactly the same as the stewards that checked our boarding passes at the airport, but sensibly enough, she seems to have swapped out the kitten heels for a pair of glossy black ballet flats. She seems quite young, really young actually, I would guess around my age from the flawless ivory baby face, and her black hair pulled back into a French plait. I couldn't imagine doing that with my life, a proper job like that so young? Surely it's almost unheard of.

The pasta is a little rubbery, but edible. The tomato sauce is clearly watered down, and the cheese is debateable, but it's not horrendous. I just wish it wasn't cold after my second mouthful. Having said that, it is like a million-dollar meal compared to what Harriet's got. It looks, smells and I'm sure tastes, absolutely foul. The meat for a start, may as well still be grazing in grasslands, and the pastry is so pale it almost looks like tracing paper. She would have paid extra for that as well, only a few meals were complimentary, and that definitely wasn't on the list; but maybe I am just not upper-class enough to enjoy such delicacies.

It was a very small portion, and probably not even half hour after I had eaten, I was reaching in my bag for the crisps. Wow, my last pack of Walkers Ready Salted.

Apparently, they have something similar called Lays in the States, but I'll just have to see if they live up to my expectations. Harriet is asleep by the time I start eating them. I don't force myself to be quiet like I normally would, after all, she woke me up, and was then dismissive and rude for no reason, not to mention, she turned her nose up at my meal as if it was peasant food.

I glance at the map she has on her screen. Wow, we really are close, we must only have a few hours left. I did take quite long eating though, and it was very chewy.

The film is mediocre; it just drags on a little more than I would have hoped, amusing though, nonetheless. I wonder what Dom will think of it? I'll have to ask him when I next speak to them both. I fully can't wait. I wonder what they are doing? We must have been up here for five-ish hours now, and the whole three-hour airport drag waiting around before boarding.

It should be around four p.m. back home, they are probably sitting down on the sofa waiting for dinner to cook, Dom probably with a beer, and Maria with a glass of wine. I bet they are watching *Tipping Point*. I can't stand the show myself, it is clearly rigged with magnets, but they both actually get the questions right on that show, so I can see the appeal.

I wonder what happened when they got back? How were they feeling? What did they decide to do with their day? It's early October, so the garden doesn't need any tending to, and it's a little too cold for a stroll round the block. Knowing Maria, she probably got straight to cleaning; she always uses it as a distraction when something bothers her, unlike Dom, who can get lost in the TV, without a care in the world. I wish I was like that.

I really hope they will be all right without me. I know it's only been a few hours, but we became so close over the years, and now, for the first time in seven years, they are back to being just a two again, and after what Dom told me the other day, I hope they don't break after this. It just feels awful to me to know that I am not there to comfort them, make them laugh and just be there if they need me. I know it will really hit Maria, we really connected, but I am happy she at least has Dom, I know he will look after her, and if they do manage to conceive a baby of their own, I know they will be just fine.

Sixteen

It was my first day with just Dom today; I would be lying, if I said I wasn't a little apprehensive. Maria had already left, I'd heard her get up and go, but I was way too tired to get up and wish her luck, I felt really guilty now. I knew I said it to her last night, but what if she had forgotten? I'll just apologise to her when she gets home, I was sure she would understand.

As I got to the bottom of the stairs, I glanced up at the silver clock hanging opposite the bannister, 10:15 a.m. I don't know why I felt so nervous it just being me and Dom; I had only ever known him when he was with Maria. What if he was a different person on his own? What if spending the whole day with me made him not like me? I really needed to step up my game today.

"Morning, Dom," I said cheerfully, as I took my seat at the table, he was sat in his usual spot on the sofa, with a plate of toast in his hands, breaking one of Maria's big rules already, no food on the furniture.

"Morning, lazy bones, I was beginning to think you had gone into hibernation up there," he said, eyes still fixed on the telly; some kind of football highlights on the screen.

"Nope, just tired I guess," I said, mimicking his blasé tone.

"You can do yourself some toast if you're hungry. It's all out there in the kitchen, everything you'll need." Still not even glancing over at me once.

"Oh, okay, yeah sounds good," I said, as I quickly walked into the kitchen, the flooring cold on my bare feet, and the air a little chilly from the open window. I had made toast a million times before, but I was a little nervous I could get this wrong. No, surely not, I could do this. I grabbed the loaf of bread, and took out the last two slices, unfortunately, only the end bits are left, not a good sign starting off the day with bad luck. I put them in the toaster, and pull the lever down, four minutes it was set to, hopefully it wouldn't burn.

I walked over to the white cabinet with the built-in fridge and took out the butter. I thought Dom had jam or something on his, but I didn't want to be rooting through the cupboards, so this would have to do, and I probably couldn't reach them properly anyway.

The toast popped up making me jump, as Dom simultaneously bellowed, "WHAT A SHOT!" at the TV.

I thinly spread the butter, quickly wiped the mess and retook my seat at the table. Forward thinking, I put the toast on a piece of kitchen role instead of a plate, less washing up for them to do later right? Good plan.

Dom still hadn't properly acknowledged me, but I preferred to eat my toast in silence. I reckoned it was probably less awkward at the moment than the latter. The toast was dry and a little bland, I may have misjudged the butter. Luckily enough, I grabbed some water when I was in the kitchen to help wash it down. The fact that it was the end part of the loaf as well, probably didn't help.

"I was thinking we could go food shopping today if you're interested?" Dom said as he finally faced me and turned the volume down on the TV, coincidentally as his programme finished. "We probably need more bread now, as it looks like you've scoffed the last of it." *Like, let's not pretend Dom, that you told me to make the toast.*

"Yeah, okay," I said shyly, avoiding eye contact. "It will be nice to see the shops round here."

"Great, well once you're ready, we can go," he said as he headed upstairs, presumably to get properly dressed himself. I mean, I couldn't see him going out in public in light grey tracksuit bottoms, and a red hoodie covered in specks of white paint.

I didn't want to make him wait, so I rushed upstairs quickly, almost stumbling onto my bed as I burst through my door full force; I hoped he didn't hear all of that.

I wanted to look nice today, so I pulled on my new blue jeans I got the other day, and one of the new tops, brushed my hair all nice and pushed it back with the Alice band. I was ready, I just needed shoes and a coat from downstairs, and we were good to go.

"You got ready quick," Dom said surprised, as he stood at the bottom of the stairs.

"Yeah, I don't like making people wait," I said reassuringly as I finally reached the bottom, waiting for him to compliment my outfit.

"Cool, let's go," he said, as I slipped into my new shoes and picked up my coat. Maria would have been obsessing over me right now, maybe he just hadn't noticed.

Dom said that Maria managed to get a lift to work this morning so he could have the car, but that we would have to pick her up later. I had wanted to see where she worked, since she first mentioned it to me. I didn't think I had actually been inside a real bank before; they were just for adults, right? And I definitely didn't have a credit card yet.

He drove a lot faster than Maria. I never really noticed it when I first came here, but compared to when we went shopping, this felt almost thrilling. He sat so far away from the steering wheel as well; it took him a good five minutes to re-adjust the seat.

Luckily enough, the shop wasn't far away. I thought we were actually quite close to the mall me and Maria went to. Dom pulled up in a bay right at the front of the store labelled, 'Parent and Child', that was kind of sweet. I guess that's what I was now, technically, their child. I couldn't help but smile as we headed into the store, Dom even said I could push the trolley if I wanted.

I had never been to a Tesco before, they're absolutely huge. A superstore was what it was called; apparently there were loads of different varieties, an express, a metro and even a Tesco Extra. How had I only ever known about a Sainsbury's?

The aisles were long and narrow, but wide enough for two trolleys to pass each other comfortably. We started right at the very left, where the vegetables and fruit were. Dom instantly picked up two bags of potatoes and three red bell peppers. I wondered if we are going to cook something tonight. We just strolled on, whilst he threw a few things in every now and then. My knowledge of vegetables wasn't quite up to scratch, so the trolley was beginning to look a little foreign to me.

"Let's get some bread," Dom said, as he picked up his pace towards a sign labelled, 'Bakery'. Wow, it smelled amazing over there, surrounded by bread, pastries, cookies, cakes, the lot. The air around me still felt a little warm from the hot food out of the ovens. Being an adult must be so hard, how were there so many different makes of bread, and not only makes, different thickness, you could get wholegrain, something called fifty/fifty and a whole 'free from' selection.

I hadn't even noticed Dom had already chosen some, until he stood there looking at me funny. A few people were to be honest, I was eyeing up everything in front of me, concentrating hard, sometimes I didn't even realise I was doing it. I guess I just liked taking everything in, especially new things.

"Right, so I know you like lasagne, so we've already got the peppers, we just need mince, a sauce and some pasta, I think we might have some left in the cupboard, but better to be safe than sorry." How could he memorise all of this? He hadn't even got a list with him.

"Okay, I think I saw a sign for pasta sauces over there," I said confidently, silently applauding my eye for detail. "And the mince must be straight ahead of us with the rest of the meat, and look there's even a little sign down there saying pasta." I felt like I had just solved some kind of puzzle, he had given me things we needed, and I found them as quickly as I could. Smashed it of course.

"Ooooo, get you!" Dom says in a very high-pitched tone. "Never been here before, but already finding your way around things. Maybe I'll write you a list next time and stay home." First time he'd smiled all morning I reckoned, but I was starting to feel more comfortable now. This was the playful Dom I was used to, now it felt normal.

With the mince, we grabbed some chicken breasts, some bacon, some sausages and a leg of lamb. I couldn't believe the prices of some of this stuff, surely it must last a while though. The trolley was almost full already, maybe we should have gone for the bigger one, and we still had so many aisles to explore.

I almost forgot where I was for a second, and I just passed by people, left right and centre, chatting away with Dom about the most random things. Maybe this was the perfect ice breaker to get us talking, sounded so silly, it wasn't like we were strangers.

"I have an idea," Dom said, as we stopped down the baking aisle. "Why don't we get one of these cupcake mixes to make for Maria for when she gets home?"

"That's a great idea!" I enthusiastically bellowed. "She would love that so much."

"All right, great! We just have a few more bits to get, and then we can head home and get stuck in."

I was so excited. What better way to show Maria that we cared, than with cakes! And what an also great way to show her how well me and Dom got on. I could tell she was a little worried, by the way she was last night, constantly reassuring us both that we would be fine alone, I think we were both having a few doubts, not that we'd ever let it show.

The smile hadn't wiped from my face since the minute Dom mentioned the idea, and we were almost home. We had been singing along to Disney songs all the way back, for a man, I was surprised he knew so many of the lyrics. Not that I was being stereotypical, but for someone who was football mad, and very macho, it was quite a shock, and yet, there I was, sat next to him, belting out 'The Circle Of Life' like his life depended on it. Imagine how amazing this would have been if Maria was here?

I had never made cupcakes before, so this should be interesting. Apparently all we needed besides the box is one egg and two tablespoons of milk, I didn't realise it could be so easy. After spending about fifteen minutes searching for the mixing bowl, Dom switched on the oven and handed me an apron. This was huge, almost down to my very toes, and was covered in flour; I wondered why he wasn't wearing one too?

"Okay, so first things first," Dom said as he studied the back of the box. "Put in sponge mix, with one medium size egg and two tablespoons of milk, then whisk till its creamy." How are you meant to determine what a medium size egg looks like! They all look the same!

Dom picked one at random, and handed it to me to break, he'd already put the sponge mix and the milk in, so I had to get this right, otherwise the whole thing would be messed up. I banged firmly on the side of the bowl, nothing. Not wanting to look stupid, I tried again, and it takes about five tries before it even started to crack a tiny bit, I hoped he didn't think I was weak; I just misjudged how hard you had to hit them.

Dom quickly whisks the mix and filled up twelve cake cases evenly, then placed them in the oven and set the timer to fifteen minutes. He said that I could decorate them all special for her, and the cake mix we got had pink icing, so I knew straight away that she would like them regardless.

I didn't realise how much mess would come out of cake making. The kitchen looked like a pig sty, and somehow there were tiny specks of cake batter all over the place. Dom said he would wash, if I dried, and to be fair, that sounded like a pretty good deal.

"So, you've never made these before?" Dom said as he filled the sink with Fairy Liquid and hot water.

"No, I haven't, I have eaten them though, lots of them," I said as he erupted into a laugh.

"I love it, very noble of you. I guess cakes definitely are a lot better, when it's not you doing the hard work." He looked at me and grins. "Just joking, your egg cracking skills, are Olympic medal material."

"Maybe I should try out next year?" I laughed, going along with his joke. It had definitely made the mood go through the roof, and for a second, I forgot what we were even doing, without even paying attention, I had dried a bowl, four spoons and a whisk, and we're pretty much done. "Thank you for today, it was nice making cakes with you," I said, as we both washed our hands.

"You don't need to thank me, and if I'm being honest, I was a little nervous about having you on my own today, like I know you're not a baby, so I wouldn't have to change nappies and stuff, but sometimes it can be weird when you still don't fully know each other yet."

"No, I completely agree," I say sharply. "I was nervous, too, I think I overthought it a bit too much, maybe we both rely on Maria more than we would like to admit," I laughed.

"Yeah, you're probably right, she definitely is the glue that holds everything together." He stopped and looked at me. "Don't tell her I said that though, I need to maintain my cool image."

"I promise I won't, as long as you don't tell her it took me six attempts to break and egg."

Dom laughed. "You have yourself a deal there!"

We were both just starting to sit down in the lounge as the oven timer chimed. Dom got up and took the cakes out the oven to cool down, he said I might as well stay where I was as this was the boring part, and I wouldn't trust myself lifting a hot tray out of the oven anyway. Last thing we both needed, was a trip to hospital to treat minor burns.

He said I could choose something for us to watch whilst we wait for the cakes to cool. I had never heard of the majority of these programmes, so I switched *SpongeBob* on, as kind of a safe choice. I was a bit worried Dom might moan about it, but oddly enough, he seemed to be enjoying it, a little too much. I bet this was what he secretly watched when Maria went out.

I think we got through three episodes or so when Dom said we'd best start decorating the cakes, as we would have to get Maria very soon. We must have lost track of time a bit. I took my seat at the dining table, as instructed, and within minutes, Dom brought me out a tray of cakes and a bowl of icing sugar. I carefully spooned a daub of the pink icing on each one, making sure it spread out evenly. The smell was delicious, must be strawberry flavour. As promised, Dom just sat back and watched, not patronisingly, but like he cared.

I sprinkled on the hundreds and thousands, and they were finished. We decided to leave them on the table, that way, Maria would see them as soon as she came in the door. I couldn't wait to see her face.

We got half way out of the door, before I realised I was still wearing my apron. Dom quickly ran it inside to make sure we didn't give away what we had done today as soon as we saw her; good thinking.

Maria greeted us both enthusiastically as she took her seat in the front of the car. One of the high street roads was closed due to a burst pipe, so we had to wait for her around the corner. I was worried that she might get confused as to what corner we were on, this place felt so much like a maze.

"So how was your day together?" Maria asked as she turned her head back and smiled at me.

"Yeah, it was all right, thanks, we went to Tesco and got some shopping for the week, and then ended up watching *SpongeBob* all afternoon," Dom said normally, like it was a usual occurrence.

"*SpongeBob*? Oh wow! Mollie, how did you manage to get him to watch that? He won't even let me watch *The Simpsons*!" Maria asked a little taken back, but playfully.

"I don't know," I laughed "Dom just said to put something on and it was the first thing I found, they were pretty good episodes though."

"Well, that's good then! And Dom, now I know you like cartoons, we can start watching my programmes as well," she said mockingly.

"Oh, Christ," Dom sniggered "You've opened a can of worms here, Moll."

We got back home, and as soon as we walked through the front door, we were greeted with a warm scent of cakes, possibly one of the best smells ever. She guessed it straight away, one foot over the threshold and she was asking us what cake we'd made today, clearly had impeccable senses.

"Oh my god! They're lovely," Maria cried as she walked in the front room and saw them waiting for her "Honestly, Mollie, that is the sweetest surprise to come home too! It really is."

"Dom did most of the cooking, but I decorated I chose pink because it's your favourite colour, we wanted to do something nice for you on your first day back at work," I say proudly as I watched her pick up a cake and take a bite.

"These are amazing, thank you, Dom, for once again proving that you are the chef of this household, and for making today that one bit more special!" Maria said in between mouthfuls.

"I bet you expected to come home to a mess today, didn't you?" Dom teased.

"To be honest, I didn't know what to expect, but I am just so glad you both had such a nice time."

"So am I, Maria, honestly, so am I," I said.

Seventeen

There it is, that seatbelt light flashing, this is it. I pull open the cover on my window, and stare breathlessly at the new ground below me. It doesn't actually look much different to England from above, but I know that what lies beneath those clouds, is a world of its own.

I can feel us starting to move downwards, my ears in absolute agony, wanting to pop, but won't. The pressure making me feel disorientated and dizzy, as I hold my nose and attempt to blow to try and clear them. It hasn't helped one bit, but I saw a couple in front of us try it, so it was worth a shot.

This is really bumpy, the feeling of us going down, is a thousand times worse than taking off — I feel like we are plummeting into the ground, and I can't see far out my window enough to at least give myself some perspective. My hands are laced with sweat, my knees shaking non-stop. Everyone around me is so calm and not even bothered, so I guess that's kinda clarification that this is all normal, right?

As the wheels hit the ground, all you can hear is a loud thud, and the piercing sound of the tires straining against the tarmac, to come to a halt. It feels nice to finally have stopped, I can't wait to just stretch my legs and breathe in some fresh air.

The stewards instruct people out of their seats, and all around me, people are grabbing hand luggage and pushing and shoving their way off of the plane. Even Harriet was one of the first people out of her seat. I think I'll wait until it gets a bit clearer, besides, these people know where they are going, they have an advantage, and heaven forbid I end up going the wrong way.

The airport is completely different to the one back home. For starters it is about four times the size with probably five thousand more people in at any given moment. There are signs absolutely everywhere saying 'Dulles International Airport' I mean, at least I know I'm in the right place, that's got to help a little right?

As I take more and more steps away from the plane, I start to feel steadier on my feet, despite the pins and needles in my legs, and the slight cramp in my left foot. I walk through an open door, following an older man in front of me for a little guidance. To my surprise, this place actually looks quite nice, it is very open planned and painted a warm breezy blue, similar to the one I had on my walls back home.

Passport control is the first hurdle, but the line is moving quickly, and I am already prepared. A man called Joey checks my documents, and within seconds I am ushered through another set of doors towards baggage claim. It seems very fast paced here, now the nerves are starting to reappear.

Baggage claim, to be fair isn't too different, but then again, how many variations of a conveyor belt system are there? This one is about four meters longer than the one back home, and is purely metal, must be extra support for heavier suitcases, I guess. Luckily enough, everyone in front of me just grabs their bags and leaves instantly, no waiting around. I see my suitcase as I approach the belt, it looks a little beaten, but I know it is my one, because I can see the purple dolphin keyring attached to the top handle, Maria's idea, not mine. I forgot I even had it to be honest.

As I lift my suitcase, all the muscles in my body cry for help. How is it this heavy? I am suddenly really grateful for Felix back in England, for lifting it for me. They should have someone like that here, it would definitely help people out, I mean, we're not all weightlifters. I should have tested the weight before leaving, but everyone else just seemed to take care of it for me, so I only actually pulled it from the car to the belt the other side, and by that point, I don't think I was feeling anything other than emotional pain.

Using all my force, I drag it onto the next part of this wonderful process. Customs. I hear the customs departments over in the states are particularly picky and strict and investigate even the smallest of things; maybe our metal detectors just aren't as thorough.

I pass my suitcase to the lady in charge, remove my shoes and place them in a plastic box for screening. As I walk through the sensors I beep, how? Instantly I have four or five people surrounding me, eyeing me up like a piece of meat.

"Excuse me, miss, do you have anything to declare?" a tall guy called Damien asks. He is definitely higher up, he is wearing a black suit with a grey tie, compared to everyone else's waistcoats and pencil trousers.

"No, I-I don't," I say stuttering with nerves.

"Right, well, would you like to walk back through then," he says with a raised eyebrow. I walk back through the sensors and there is the same beep again. What the hell is that! I don't have anything on me that I shouldn't have! And I took my earrings out last night to avoid this exact thing happening.

Two of the men look at each other and share a nod, and with that, I feel two hands on my shoulders, and am being lightly pushed into a room by Damien.

"Hi, my name's Damien, this is my colleague Charlie, and we would like to ask you a few questions if you wouldn't mind?" Not exactly like I have a choice is it? This room is plain with white walls, no windows at all, it's a little claustrophobic. A small desk sits in the middle of the room with three chairs, I take my seat opposite them, my whole body shaking. I know I don't have anything on me, but my body language I reckon would suggest otherwise. I nod agreeing to the questions, there isn't much else of an option, and standing directly behind me is a security guard, all kitted out and dressed in black holding a gun. I want to go home.

"Could you please state loudly for the tape your full name and date of birth," Damien says as he studies my passport and then my face, and what tape? Where is this tape?

"Erm yeah, my name is Mollie Fitzgerald, my date of birth is the 23rd September 1999." It's funny, I know that information perfectly, but suddenly I am second guessing my whole existence.

"Okay, Mollie," Damien says, still studying my documents. He doesn't look as tall and scary now he's sat down, but Charlie on the other hand, has piercing eyes that I feel can see deep into my soul, and a bald head. Damien's hair situation isn't much better to be honest; I didn't know comb overs were still a thing. There is a slight pause before he continues, "So where have you travelled from today Mollie?" I hate it when people keep using my name in sentences, it's like they do it to try and enforce dominance, it happened all the time at high school.

"I have come from England, sir," regaining a bit more of myself back, to be able to answer him sufficiently. "Gatwick Airport."

"I see," he says, then nothing. Charlie on the other hand still hasn't removed his eye contact once. "What are you doing over here in the States, Mollie?" Damien continues.

"I have a place at Jaystead, I have never flown before so this is my first time out of the country, I am here to study Law." Not that he asked for my life story, but the more details I feel I give, the less questions he might have to ask.

Charlie pulls out a walkie-talkie from thin air, and radios through to someone. "Charlie to control — could you get Simon to ring up Jaystead and see if they are expecting a Mollie Fitzgerald." Someone on the other side says okay and here we are again, silence. Why do they need to ring campus? What an awful impression this is going to make! They've never met me in person, but have border control asking questions about me, like that will help solve why the stupid sensors beeped.

"So you are studying law, you say? So you must be aware why we have pulled you back here," Damien says studying me closely.

"A little," I say, "I mean, I know it's because the metal detector went off, but I have no idea why," I say a little to sternly. My tone is picked up immediately by Charlie, who throws me the most daring look.

"Basically, yes," Damien starts, "Obviously you are here for the machine beep, but also the fact that you are only nineteen, and travelling alone for the first time on a blank British passport, to go to a university thousands of miles away, seems a little fishy to us. Usually we would expect to see one or two other journeys stamped in your passport." Looks like Dom's ingenious plan to save money really paid off.

"Oh, right, yeah, I see your point," I say sympathetically, trying to get some reason with him. I've given up with Charlie, I have already decided he hates me so no point trying to win him over. "Basically, I have been living with foster parents for the past seven years, and obviously money is extremely tight. My foster dad," it just seems easier to refer to them as that at this point, "set up online interviews with the educational board over here, and I was able to complete my application that way, rather than having to physically come all the way out here." Saying it out loud, it actually sounds so ridiculous. Yeah, trust me officers, I phoned the campus and they gave me a space, hardly believable. But to my luck Charlie's radio chimes the best message I think I have ever heard.

"This is Simon to Charlie; campus has confirmed suspect is a new student there, staying in dorm 301." Silence again, before Charlie replies a brisk, "Thanks."

"All right," Damien says, "But we still need to perform a strip-search because of the alarm. Now, because you are nineteen, do you give us consent to do this?" What kind of question is that? Like I am going to say no! Just the thought alone is sending shivers all the way down my spine; I don't ever want to strip for anyone, let alone three strange men. With that being said I stand up slowly, and to my luck the men exit and a woman appears, Melanie, her name is, judging by her name tag. She is short and overly chubby, dark skinned with short brown hair tucked behind her purple glasses. She is definitely intimidating, but rather her than them.

After a quick wand search, with no beeping or cause for concern, she steps back. "Okay, miss, I am going to need you to remove all items of clothing and place them in this box on the table." She speaks with a croaky voice, but one that would frighten me if ever raised into a shout. She pulls rubber gloves on her hands, and stands to face me. How is there not a special place for this with more room? I slip off my leggings quickly and my socks, placing them in the box as instructed, as I start to take off my cardigan, I hear a faint rustle, and to my feet drops a small piece of foil from the fruit pastel packet. Melanie, looks at me, and then down at the floor four or five times before speaking. I just stand here like a statue, waiting for whatever is to come next. "Could you please redress yourself, ma'am," she says as she bends down, picks it up and puts it in a little zip lock bag. I hope they don't think I have tried to smuggle drugs.

She leaves, and a few moments pass before Damien and Charlie return with the guard, who, I suspect has been waiting outside the door this whole time.

"So, Mollie, obviously as you know we have found something, care to elaborate what it is?" Damien asks abruptly, sitting in his chair, body dead straight, like this is his serious side.

"Yeah," I say, "I brought some fruit pastels in England before boarding the plane, and when I was eating them on the flight, a piece of the wrapper must have stuck to me," again, not sounding convincing. I swear, when I get out of here, I am practicing my people skills.

"Okay, so taking your word for it, obviously it is currently being tested with our forensics, so if they find nothing but sugar traces, you can go." How can it be that easy? I mean, obviously, the foil is an absolute life saver, which proves my innocence completely, but surely there must be more steps for something as thorough as this? I was almost naked and searched for God's sake!

"All right," I say, deciding to just go along with whatever they say.

"First, before any of that, now we have taken the sample, and your jacket has been inspected by my colleague, Melanie, with nothing else found, we would like you to walk back through the sensors, and if nothing goes off, then like I said, you will be free to go as long as the results come back in your favour. If not, then we will have to finish carrying out the search, is that okay?" Sounds pretty fair to be honest and I know the results will be fine, so let's just cross our fingers that it was the foil that made the machine go off.

As I walk over, escorted by both men and the guard, I can feel people's eyes on me, people whispering and staring pathetically at a young girl, for all they know, being caught for drug trafficking or something. I walk through the sensors, and not one sound. I let out a loud,

"YES!" as I turn to face the guards, clearly unamused by my cheering, I step to the side and let the people waiting, carry out their checks, as Melanie appears in front of me and whispers something to Damien and walks away, and with the coldest look on his face, he has me walk back over to that room.

"Okay, Mollie, just a few things for paperwork reasons, I just need you to sign a few things for me," he sounds polite and genuine this time.

"Does this mean I am free to go?" I ask hopefully

"Yes," he says. "First time we have ever almost searched a teenager over a sweet wrapper, but at least we know our machines are top of the range."

Charlie lets out a laugh, wow, who knew he could show any kind of emotion? And I think we all agree on the how ridiculous the extent of this situation is. Maybe they really are nice guys deep down, but they have to be mean and scary to intimidate real suspects into confessing, and it was the first time he spoke without using my name, I think we are making progress.

You would be surprised the amount of paperwork that goes into detaining and then releasing someone for the amount of people they must stop every day. Just walking out of there I saw two people being directed into a room the same as I was. I wonder what sweets they ate on the plane?

Eighteen

The morning was going just as smoothly as every other Sunday, Disney film with Maria whilst Dom slept, heavenly pancakes for breakfast, by popular request, and a planned pyjama day ahead.

I'd put on my Sesame Street ones, last night, ready for today. Don't get me wrong, I loved the other ones, but it just felt more meaningful when I wore these ones, especially when we were all together like this. Maria said that she wished they had done them in adult sizes, whilst Dom joked that I may as well just live in them forever. I wish.

It was nice to have a 'family' day as they called it, no reason for anyone to need to go anywhere, no washing or cleaning to do, because Maria got it all done on Saturdays ready; again, always planning. They both said that a Sunday was always the best day to relax, because one of them would always have to work Monday morning, made total sense.

"What popcorn would you like, Molls?" Dom shouted from the kitchen, as me and Maria get snuggled up on the sofa under a blanket each.

"Sweet please, Dom," I shouted back timidly, but loud enough for him to hear.

"Here you go," he said, as he strutted in and threw me the bag. He and Maria preferred salted, but like they said, just meant more for me at the end of the day; result.

"Thanks," I replied sweetly.

It was Dom's turn to choose the film today, and to be honest, I think me and Maria were both a little bit worried as to what we might get stuck with, that, and the fact that his indecisiveness made everything so much longer.

Thankfully, he picked Chicken Little. Maria seemed surprised by that one, again, apparently, he had never been a big cartoon fan, but I reckoned, secretly it was his guilty pleasure, and if he used me as an excuse to watch them with us, I'd gladly play along.

It is still hot outside for the most part, although it was starting to slowly cool down day by day, I was looking forward to the winter, they'd both said it was their favourite time of year, and I was intrigued to find out why.

The film was just as mesmerising as the first time I ever watched it. I loved the animation, especially on a film that came out quite a while ago, and being truthful, I was in love with his little green glasses. It was funny, the first time I'd seen this, I didn't fully understand the plotline, and even now, I'm looking at the screen and some parts just went straight over my head. The whole spaceship part just confused me, but the rest was all good.

It got me thinking, I wonder if Maria and Dominic would be there for me if I were saying something so out of the ordinary, for example, if I had a premonition that the sky was falling, would they believe me? I would hope so, because like this movie proves, sometimes your instincts or visions can be true, no matter how bizarre, and sometimes you just needed one person to have your back.

"So, Mollie," Maria said as she shut off the TV, and they both turned to face me. The room, a little darker now, as rain clouds hovered up above the house. Dom said last night that it was predicted to rain, but that it was also the best weather for a movie day because you were more in the mood to snuggle up and get cosy. "You turn thirteen in two weeks, that's exciting." She was smiling at me intensely, as if to try and read my thoughts before I had a chance to say them, just in case they were not positive.

"Oh right, yeah, I guess so," I said, staring at this month's copy of *OK!* magazine on the table.

"What would you like to do for it?" she continued. "I know we don't live too local to anything that interesting, but we can always drive somewhere further."

"I'm not too sure," I said.

"What have you previously done for your birthdays?" Dom asked, mirroring both our tones, keeping the conversation flowing the same way.

"Well, funnily enough, I have never had a birthday whilst in a placement. Anytime I have been moved, it has been directly after it, or it finishes just before. Which is fine, obviously, I mean, we did some stuff at the home too."

"Oh really, like what?" Maria said as she leaned forwards and put her hands on her knees, obviously fishing for some clues.

"Well, being in the home, there was never a big budget, so birthdays were celebrated quarterly, anyone who had a birthday in each four-month span at a time, would be allowed to go to a little disco held in the rec room, the same one I met you in."

"I wondered why there was a disco ball in the corner," Dom chuckled.

"Let her finish," Maria replied softly, as she nodded at me to continue.

"Seeing as my birthday is November, it was always quite busy at my disco. They didn't last very long, and we would always listen to the same CD on loop for two hours, but it was a time to go crazy, and let loose, and at one point, when I was about eight or nine, I really relaxed and let myself go, haven't had a stitch as big as that in forever." I could feel a smile spreading on my face as I began to remember, the lights, the music, people genuinely having a good time and celebrating with us all, no cares in the world.

"Well that sounds fun," Maria said, trying not to sound quite as disheartened by what she had just heard.

"Tell me about your best birthdays and maybe we can do something like that?" I said, as I stared at them both, my eyes full of optimism. This was clearly important to them, and would also give me a better idea of their likes and dislikes.

"That's easy," Maria smiled. "My best birthday would have to be my fifteenth. My parents took me and a few close friends to 'Sandy Adventure Land'. It's long been closed down now, though. It was the most amazing theme park you could ever imagine, hundreds of rides on acres of land to accommodate all age groups. That's why we chose it, it's always nice to have something for everyone." I admired that, even on a day that was meant to be just for her benefit, she thought of other people as well. "It was such a sunny day too," she continued. "I remember getting a brand new sweatshirt as a gift, and refused to take it off the whole time we were there, didn't half drive my parents mad, but I wasn't bothered about the possibility of sunstroke, I was having way too much fun. There was this one ride called 'The Spinning Machine' and you basically sat in a seat in pairs, and were spun around so fast, whilst being thrown in the air in every direction, me and my friend Jenny went on it so many times, we were both sick when we got home. It was so worth it." It was so nice sitting here, watching her smile as she delved deep into her mind to remember such a happy time. "And when the day was over, we had the most amazing dinner at a little restaurant on the way home, and the waiters and everyone sang to me, was such a sweet moment. I think I remember that one so much because that was the last time I saw Jenny. She relocated to New Zealand because her dad got a new job. I don't think I have ever cried so much in my life." Maybe that's why Maria is so nice and understanding of what I had been through. I knew she was paying close attention the other day when I was telling her about Chloe, because in a similar way, she had been through something like that too, I felt like we could relate to each other.

"What about you, Dom," I said softly.

"Erm, I would say my seventeenth, I went paintballing with nine other mates and we just destroyed each other! I don't think I have ever had so many bruises in my life, we were all black and blue the next day, was a proper laugh though." He, like Maria, smiled all way through telling his, but unsurprisingly, that was all he had to say about it. Men definitely do have a different way of speaking than women, no emotions involved, just a brief description of probably one of the funniest things he had ever done, and judging by his smirk, there is a lot more to the story inside his mind. It's all right though, I'd pull it out of him one day.

"Wow," I said, more aimed at Maria, "How eventful! It's great you both still have those memories!"

"That's what we want for you love, we wanna do it properly this year." I'm a little taken back by this for a second, it hadn't even been two months since I'd got there, and they already wanted to make special memories with me, it really was touching.

"What about the zoo?" Dom suggested as he wrapped his blanket tighter around his legs. "We have one not that far from here and we both haven't been in ages."

Maria's eyes lit up instantly at that suggestion and on that alone, I was won over, it must be pretty life changing to see all those animals in real life!

"Oh my god, I would love that," I said, probably more excited than I had ever been before. "If that is okay with you as well, Maria?" I asked as I gave her a hopeful smile, but not one that would make her feel pressured to say yes.

"I think that is a great idea, the zoo is a lovely day out, and, with it being November, it shouldn't be too busy! Just hope it doesn't rain."

I loved that we were already coming up with things to look forward to, and I loved how invested they were in me, and I fully could not wait for my birthday this year, and I didn't think I had ever been able to say that before, maybe this really was what I had been looking for.

Nineteen

I feel so relieved to feel the fresh air hit my face again, as I take my first steps out of the airport, a place I would be happy to never visit ever again. There must be other airports around here for me to fly home from, because that is what is keeping me going at the moment, the fact that I know deep down, if I absolutely hate it here, that I can go back home. I just have to try at least.

People all around me are getting into cars, on buses and I think I even saw a minibus just drive off. Lucky for me, Dom painted me a picture in my head as to where I go now, and the most important thing to do; don't panic.

I hear someone emerge from behind me talking about catching an Uber, so without even thinking, I grasp my bag and follow. That has probably saved me a load of time, I wonder how long they wait for you? Because with my questioning, it must have been well over an hour now since landing. I'm starting to realise quickly why Dom said to have money with you straight away.

It actually looks like something out of a movie, hundreds of cars all lined up, waiting for their passengers. I quickly see someone standing at the far end, holding a white sign. My instincts tell me instantly that he is probably waiting for me, it also seems like something Dom would have arranged to help me in case I have a 'Mollie moment', as Dom would always say.

As I get closer, I can make out my name on his sign, surely that isn't safe? Like anyone could walk over and claim to be me, and not only that, now everyone knows my name and the fact that I will be going off in that car. People must have more trust of strangers over here. In England, it would all be manic with identify theft and all sorts, especially at an airport. I hope he doesn't ask for ID, I slid my passport through a gap in my suitcase whilst walking outside, seemed like a more sensible place to keep it without getting lost.

"Hi, I'm Mollie," I say anxiously as I approach him slowly.

"Hi, Mollie, my name is Tobi, I'll put your bag in the back if you want to hop in the front." Is that it? No checks or anything, just taking my word for it? Fair enough, I guess even if it was the wrong person and he took them somewhere else, he would still get paid.

The car is very comfortable, but maybe I am just too tired to pay attention to anything else. I didn't get a chance to check what car it was, major fail there, Maria always said to make a note of the reg and car if getting into a strange vehicle, just in case something happens, but I'm just gonna put all my faith in Tobi not to kidnap me. I think when we Googled it back home, we found out that the journey from the airport is about an hour and a half, not enough time to sleep, but too much time to have to stay awake, my eyelids feel like they have paper cuts.

So far, looking out my window, it doesn't look massively different, besides being on the other side of the road of course. It's nice to not be stuck at traffic lights on every corner though; 'STOP' signs are definitely more efficient. The weather here is pretty gloomy, and if we landed about seven p.m. British time, another hour in the airport, and the fact Washington is five hours behind, it must be around three p.m. right now here. Wow, that took a lot more working out in my head than it probably needed to.

I'm quite happy with my choice of outfit, now more than ever. I was a little worried it would be really cold here, but to be honest, it's no different than it was back home, always good to find similarities.

"So, Mollie," Tobi says, breaking the silence. He is very pale skinned with mullet-style dirty blonde hair, wearing a grey t-shirt that says 'BORN IN THE USA' across the front and bright blue flared jeans, topped off with some chunky white trainers. "Where have you travelled from?"

"England," I stutter. "I have never been abroad before, this is my first time."

"Oh, really," His voice is quite raspy; I would guess straight away that he is probably a heavy smoker. "First time abroad and you're moving somewhere pretty permanent." I wonder what he means by that? I mean, I know I will probably be here, provided everything goes well, for about three or four years, longer if I choose, but I don't plan on staying here any longer than I need to, nothing against the United States, but I would much rather stay in England forever.

"Yeah, I guess I never really thought of it like that," I say, continuing the small talk. "I just think I'm gonna take every day as it comes, it's gonna be scary, but will hopefully be so worth it in the end." My eyes focus out my passenger window, as we go through small towns, and then highways almost concurrently. I start to feel nauseous again. I wonder if that's because of sleep deprivation or just flat out fear, I need to divert my mind. "So how long have you been a driver for?" I ask, completely changing the subject.

"Twelve years," he says bluntly. "I used to work in a factory making women's clothes not far from here actually," like I have any idea where we are. "I got laid off, most of us did, they have machines for most of it now, so we just weren't needed any more."

"Oh, that sucks," I say genuinely.

"Yeah, I had worked there since I left school, so I had no experience in any other field. It took me ages to find a job afterwards, but like I'm sure you can imagine, you don't need much in the way of qualifications to drive a car."

"No, I guess you're right," I say slowly, becoming more and more aware that I am, in fact, still with a strange man.

"Don't look too afraid," he lets out a laugh that quickly develops into a chesty cough "I have been through all the necessary checks to do this."

"Oh, of course," I say. "You wouldn't be able to do it otherwise."

The conversation pretty much dies there and then, and for a good five or ten minutes, we are in complete silence, Tobi glancing over at me every now and then, which only makes things more awkward.

"I'll tell you what," he says very confidently, breaking the silence like glass shattering everywhere in a museum of mirrors. "I'll tell you about myself, and then I won't seem so scary." How have I made it so obvious?

"Okay," I say nervously, silently hoping that this will work.

"So, you already know my name, my job history and that I am an amazing driver." He looks over and flashes a small smile "I am fifty-three years of age, but I know, I know, I look about thirty." I let out a little laugh, instantly getting rid of the elephant in the car with us. "I'm happily married to a beautiful woman called Joy, we share the same birthday, and also share three children, Michael, Tony and Vincent. Of course, they're all adults now, so it's mainly just us two at home."

"Three boys," I say interrupting. "You must have had your hands full."

"No, they're good kids to be fair, they have their moments, but I'm proud of who they are now. It's all down to Joy of course, she keeps them grounded, you know? Always making sure they're doing the right thing."

"That's sweet; you must have a great connection."

"Oh yeah, she's my rock."

All of this just instantly reminds me of Maria and Dom, and how they have both said to me on so many occasions, that they're both each other's shoulder to lean on. I know they still have a little way to go until they're in their fifties, but I have faith they will go all the way, babies or no babies. I have never seen a love like that before.

"That's lovely," I say, truly meaning my words. "I guess I better introduce myself too then, seeing as you just shared your life." Starting to feel more comfortable by the second, so why not share something about myself, I mean, if he's a kidnapper, then he will take me anyway, might as well pass the time. I do feel less like he is a threat to me now, though. I notice he has a tattoo on his right hand saying 'Joy' so at least I know his story is true. Damn, I really need to stop analysing people so much.

"Ok, Mollie, go for it," he says calmly.

"Well, to give you the short version, my mother died when I was born and I was immediately put into a care home, I had six placements through the years, up until I was twelve, when a lovely couple called Maria and Dominic welcomed me into their home, and I have lived with them ever since. I always wanted to study law, and I think watching too much TV convinced me the US was the best place to get my degree. It all seemed like a good idea right up until a few weeks ago, when I finally realised what I have got myself into." My words flow easily, and without error. I must be speaking a little quiet though, because Tobi keeps leaning into me slightly cupping his ear to hear better. Noticing it, I slightly raise my voice. "Like I said, I have never been abroad, especially nowhere this far away, and the only communication with the university I have had, has been video chat, which even then gave me no insight into what my life will be like there." I get a shiver down my spine just talking about it, like, where the hell, am I going?

"Don't feel too disheartened, I actually live about five minutes away from campus, that's why they chose me for this pick-up. I don't tend to drive too far, but since you were going somewhere so close, I didn't mind making a day out of it," Tobi says softly.

"Can you tell me anything about it?" I say, trying to mask my desperation. "What is it like?"

"It's a very beautiful campus, one of the prettiest I have seen in terms of appearance. Our boys all went there when they graduated high school and we never had any problems. The staff that we connected with during those years were all very polite, and you will be pleased to know that nothing bad really happens there. Not that in other places it's dangerous, but you hardly ever see Jaystead's name on news reports."

"Oh right," I say, obviously relieved. "That's good to know."

"You've done really well to get in there, they don't accept many people from overseas unless they are exceptionally smart. I would say, one or two a year if that. They like to give their spaces to people in the district mainly, the only place that really cares about that. I guess they have more chance of committing to schedules and finishing the courses if they live nearby." Like I needed more of a reason to feel like an outcast, not that I gave it much thought, but I guess I just assumed that the place would be full of people from different countries like myself. Must just be another 'Mollie moment'.

Twenty

It was my birthday the next day, and Maria and Dom had been tiptoeing around in secret for the past few days. I hoped they didn't go through too much fuss just for me. I knew they wanted it to be special, but it would be, just by being with them, not in a soppy way, but the first time I'd actually had a plan made for my birthday, and after all, I was finally becoming a teenager. I didn't know if I was happy or sad about that. I felt like when you hit your teens, that was it, your childhood was over, you were becoming an adult now, or as close to it as you could get. Made me a little bit more apprehensive about Maria's high school suggestion, I bet people were so much more grown up than me there, I mean, not even a month ago, I'd been skipping heartbeats over a keyring.

Apparently, Dom was taking me to the cinema this afternoon whilst Maria cleaned the already spotless house. It didn't really take a genius to guess what she wanted me out of the way for. But still, I was excited for the day planned; Dom said we were going to see a movie called, *Wreck-it Ralph*, coincidentally another cartoon! It did look pretty good to be fair, he showed me a trailer for it last night, something about a character from a game going into other people's games and sabotaging them, well that's what I thought I saw happening anyway, was quite hard with Dom's cracked phone screen; but we made do.

At 10:52 a.m., I can hear Maria hoovering downstairs. She always got up early to hoover, probably because it took her a good hour or two. I had never known anyone to be so thorough with something like that before, but I loved living in such a clean house.

The film didn't actually start until three p.m., so I decided I was just going to lay there for a while. Surprisingly, I was not hungry, which made a change. Usually I was woken up by the mattress vibrating from my starving tummy, but not today, probably had something to do with all of that chocolate I ate last night, I felt pretty sick afterwards, but believe me when I tell you, it was so worth it.

I felt like my room was really starting to come together now, it looked like someone sleeps in it now, I kinda missed it being so perfect, but I also loved that this room just screamed my name. Shoes on the floor and clean washing in a pile ready to be put away. Maria was going to do it, but I said I would to give her one less job to do. I really needed to get round to that.

It was so nice to see the sleeves of my cardigans poking out of the wardrobe, and my dressing gown hanging on the bathroom door handle, and my hairbrush sat next to me on my bedside table, just where I liked to keep it. I had never really had this before, even in placements. I was always sharing with at least one other person, not that I was complaining, but it was nice to have something that is just mine.

"Hello, lazy monkey," Maria said jokingly as she opened my door to drop off some more clean washing, I couldn't even look at her as I saw her notice the other pile still there from a few days ago, I hoped she wasn't mad at me. "I can help you put all these clothes away if you would like."

"Oh, no, that's okay, thank you," I said a little honeyed. "I was actually just going to do that this morning, I thought I would leave it until today, so I had something to do so I wouldn't be disturbing you cleaning downstairs." What the hell had just come out of my mouth? Not only had I made up some flat lie, I had also insinuated that Maria liked peace and quiet when she cleaned. I hoped she hadn't taken that in the wrong way; actually, if I was hoping for things, I hoped she wasn't even listening.

"I like that kind of thinking, very practical." She smiled at me. "Well I'd better leave you to it then, looks like you have a lot of work to do." She closed my door and headed downstairs. I couldn't tell if she was being sarcastic or not? But I swung my legs over the edge of the bed and stood up quicker than I have done anything in my life.

I took a seat on my floor and decided it was best to sort everything into categories. Maria spent ages getting my drawers perfect, and I couldn't even bear to think about the shame of putting a top in the trousers drawer.

The pile wasn't as scary now I was up close to it. I forget sometimes that I really didn't have too many clothes. I thought it was the jumpers folded up that made it look huge. I silently chuckled to myself in my head, thinking, if only they could both see me now, Dom would probably be laughing at how long it had taken me to make five piles, whilst Maria would probably defend herself saying that she knew I would use the floor for something. It was so weird how much information about people's personalities that you could pick up in such a short time.

As I stood up, both of my knees clicked loudly, and my shoulders started to ache. Wow, I guess turning thirteen tomorrow really was creeping up on me. I placed everything in the correct drawers and hung the jumpers up in my wardrobe, wasn't hard at all; mind blown. I did a little spin on the spot, taking a look at the rest of the room. How great would it be if I just made the whole thing immaculate? That would make up for the mess Maria had seen this morning for sure!

I started with the shoes, the whole two pairs. I shouldn't really have had them up here, but they both didn't seem to care. I placed them at the bottom of my wardrobe and closed the door; another thing accomplished. All that was left was to make my bed, and put the dirty clothes from yesterday in the hamper. Surely it could have been worse right? My room was a pretty decent size, so in the bigger picture, it probably was hardly noticeable.

Like a kid in a candy shop, I rushed downstairs to get Maria to come and look at my progress. As I hit the bottom step, she came rushing over to me in a panic. I guess I was running down them pretty fast. She followed me upstairs, and I even decided to grab Dom on the way; why not let us all mask in my glorious efforts.

"Okay, so, I know you may have noticed that my room was starting to look a little sloppy," I said as I faced them both, the three of us just stood outside my bedroom door in a line.

"It wasn't that bad," Maria laughed as she nudged Dom on the shoulder to join in.

"Oh, right, yeah," he said, mid-yawn "No, I think your room looked fine, Molls, why? What have you done to it?"

Trying not to add any more suspense, I pushed the door open and ushered them both inside, a smile gleaming off my face as they both looked around for a few minutes in silence.

"Bloody hell, Moll, looks just like it did when you first came here, minus all the teddies of course," Dom said as he winked at me.

"How have you managed to do that so quickly," Maria gasped, clearly remembering the state she had seen it in half hour ago. I wondered if she really meant that or if she was just trying to humour me because I was still young, so any effort at all was to be appreciated.

"Well," I begin, "as we all know, it's my birthday tomorrow, and I want to start taking some responsibility for myself, this is my room so I want to take care of it by myself," I said proudly, as I too, stared around the room with a smile at how nice it now looked. I knew it was only a few bits lying around, but I saw what people now mean, when they say there was no better feeling than having a clean room. Also I thought that maybe because I done it, I was giving myself more brownie points in my head as a reward, because technically, a monkey could have done it, but they hadn't, I had, and it was the first time I had been able to show them that I could do something productive by myself since I had come here.

"How lovely," Maria said, as she put her arm around my left shoulder. "It looks fantastic, maybe you can give Dom a lesson on housework, for some reason his laundry still ends up on the floor right next to the hamper." You could tell she was being playful, but that look in her eye showed that she meant every word, like a little sly dig, I loved it.

"Oh, babe, please, we know you love cleaning, last time I tried to do anything, it set your OCD off so bad that you had to reorganise the whole bedroom."

"Yeah, that's true, actually," she said as she grinned at him. "Best to stay away from the cleaning side of things, Dom, us girls can take over, you just worry about cooking us up some lunch."

"That I can do," he said as he headed downstairs, me and Maria in tow. Had we just made up our own routine?

Twenty-one

I have tried to pretend that I haven't seen the signs for Jaystead for about five miles now, out of sight, out of mind. But now as we pull over outside a set of black iron gates, I know this really is it. I don't want to get out of the car, I feel comfortable sitting here with Tobi, and I kinda now trust him, I hope everyone is as nice as he is.

"Well," Tobi starts, "this is the end of the line Miss Mollie, you ready for that adventure?" He gives me a reassuring look as he takes off his seatbelt and opens his door. I do the same, without much thought, I feel frozen. I don't know why I thought the airport would be the hardest part, because this is a whole new world. With homes, it was different, because they wanted you and accepted you, but here is a whole new ball game, you have to make yourself fit in, and what if I'm just not up to the task.

"I guess so," I say meeting him at the boot of the car and steadying myself once again with my beloved suitcase, my new favourite thing in the world.

"Well, good luck with everything, here's my card if you ever need a lift somewhere, or back to the airport." He gives me a wink, I say thank you, and with that, he drives away. I'm stuck here.

I walk through the gates, every bone in my body trembling, I could faint. I see herds of people up ahead, almost like a swarm, my feet clinging to the grey tiles with every step. The narrow path goes along straight ahead for as far as I can see, with bright green fields either side full of pretty trees and park benches.

In a weird way the air feels different here, thinner, if that makes sense, cleaner. Perhaps just because I am now around so much nature, but it will be a great place to do some reading once I'm settled in. Settled in? Blimey, I'm making plans here already, can't say I'm surprised, though. I pretty much planned my whole life out with Maria and Dom the moment I first met them. I really need to learn to not get my expectations up so high, I reckon Maria and Dom were just a lucky fluke.

As I get closer to everything, I start to see tables lined up along the path closer to the pale grey, rustic building standing powerfully in front of me. I have seen something like this in movies, different clubs trying to get you to sign up to things like cheerleading and maths club. Nothing like that for me right now, I can't be dealing with small talk. I just need to know where I need to go, to get there, and try and relax.

I keep my head down as I walk deeper and deeper into the crowd, not looking up once, keeping myself to myself, almost as if I feel like this makes me invisible. I wish. There are all sorts of loud noises bellowing around me, filling my body with tension, as the sound waves cocoon me like a caterpillar, who isn't ready to develop and become something new yet.

I remember watching a movie called *Sydney White* with Maria a few years ago, that was all about legacies and sorority houses, which I kind of had an inkling would still be about today, but I didn't think it would be like this.

On every table, is a different sorority wearing a different colour, waiting to enrol their new applicants, I guess this is something I will need to remember;

Pink, Kappa Seals (Full of bleach blonde Barbie girls with lip fillers)

Blue, Kappa Martians (Full of very muscly teenage boys wearing fake tan and holding a rugby ball — well, I guess that's a football over here)

Green, Kappa Kennedy (Full of math nerds, holding calculators and wearing 'Geometry Rocks' t-shirts, that they seem to be giving to every new recruit)

Orange, Kappa Zeus (Full of what in England we would call emos fully dressed in black)

Makes sense that I am going to be in some regular dorm, probably miles away from anything decent, because I don't fit into any of those categories, and proudly so. Also, the fact that there is not even a tiny chance in hell that I could be a pledge.

All I can picture in my head, as I walk past these people — who are judging me silently, you can tell, teens don't have the best ability to hide facial expressions — I feel like I have just been dropped into a scene of *Mean Girls*.

To reach the end of that walk of shame was a relief, I'm not going to lie, and also, I can finally hear myself think again. Not like they are very nice thoughts though, more so in the way of wanting to turn around and run back through the gates, but I guess I have to try a little harder.

"Hi, are you new here?" I hear behind me as someone approaches me at top speed.

"Erm yeah, what gave it away? The suitcase or the fear in my eyes?" I reply bluntly

"Great, well my name is Connie. I'm in my last year here, and a bunch of us have been chosen to help the freshers by showing them where to go," she says in the same over enthusiastic tone, almost bypassing my standoffishness completely. She, funnily enough, is wearing the exact same sweater Maria brought me. Maybe I should have worn that instead, it would make me blend in a bit better.

"Oh right, okay, cool," I say, hoping that this conversation is actually going somewhere, and that I am closer to being settled in. She hands me a map, which just looks too confusing to even try and figure out right now, so I just shove it in my pocket without thought.

"If you would like to follow me, I will show you where you check in. I take it you're not in one of the sororities," she says as she looks at me up and down, almost in disgust, obviously no match for her expensive Wrangler blue jeans, and Calvin Klein glasses.

"No, I'm not," I say, choosing to just go along with it. "I came here from England," as if that might speed things up a little bit. Like Tobi said, they rarely have people from overseas, so there must be some kind of special arrangements set up.

"Ah, I see," she says as we start to head towards the white steps leading into the building. It feels like a palace, windows nicely spaced out all over the brick wall, and a beautiful arch just above the stairs. This is the kind of place you would want to get married; it all feels so posh and well-taken care of, which, for a university, must be a pretty tough job, considering the amount of mess they must get here. Just walking in, I saw three bins overflowing, and that's not even half of it.

The corridor, as soon as you walk in, is painted a snowy white colour, with picture frames lacing the walls of random people, I guess maybe head students or something? The light-grey, hardwood floor gleams elegantly as the light reflects off the gloss from the huge chandeliers. This really is a picture to behold.

"So, you will be in the Hope dorm, with our other foreign students," Connie says, as we proceed to walk down the long corridor, barely anyone else in here, just one or two other people minding their own business, everyone else must be back out there enjoying the fun.

"Okay," I reply slowly. "I didn't realise there was a specific dorm for people from overseas," and I didn't realise I would now be referred to as a foreigner.

"Well, technically, it's not a proper dorm, we just call it one because it's easier. It's the top floor of the western building, with about four rooms, each with about two or three other roommates in. The principal thought it would be best to keep you all together, might make you settle in quicker, knowing someone else is going through the same thing." I understand that, but still, I think, I would rather be mixed with others, rather than being known solely for being from another country.

"Oh right, so it's just girls in the dorm?" I ask, praying that she says yes.

"Yeah, boys and girls aren't really supposed to mix, except in the sororities, they can't really do much about it there, especially since the legacies pay for the houses themselves." I didn't realise they had to pay, mind you, someone has to.

We reach the end of the corridor, and turn left into a huge room full of different tables, all with people wearing that same sweater as Connie behind them.

"Okay, so from here for you it is pretty simple. Go through these tables one by one where you will get all your information and everything you need. You might need to get your passport out though just to verify who you are, the western building is just through that back door," she says pointing behind us. "That tall grey one right there, I hope you settle in well here with us," and she was gone.

My biggest problem at the moment was trying to figure how to get my passport out of this suitcase without the whole thing bursting open, whilst also trying to attract the least amount of attention possible to myself in the process. I am way too jet-lagged for this.

I would say after about fifteen minutes of forcefully shoving my hand through a gap in the zip and rummaging as carefully as I can, I finally find it. Not ideal that my hand is now red raw from the friction, but a goal accomplished nonetheless.

I walk over to the first table.

"Hi, welcome to Jaystead, my name is Liam, can I start by taking your full name."

"Yeah, sure," I say, still a little flustered from all of that faffing about. "My name is Mollie Fitzgerald, I'm here from England." Jeez, for someone who doesn't want to draw attention to their nationality, I seem to have a problem with being able to not tell people as soon as we meet. Typical; I may as well just have worn an 'I love the UK' t-shirt.

"Okay, Mollie, nice to meet you," he says smiling, as if he hasn't already done this same process hundreds of times today, but still, I appreciate his devotion. "I see here that you are staying in the Hope dorm, room 370. When you go to the next table you will get your key and welcome pack." How amazing that back home, my door number was 370, and now I have the same one here, maybe this is meant to be? "I have marked you in as arrived for our systems, and you will find out more as you progress." He smiles and instantly starts talking to a small brown-haired girl behind me. I don't know what I'm more annoyed about, the fact that he was so nice and then just dismissed me completely, or the fact that I didn't actually need my passport!

The next station, like he said was a key and a welcome pack. It came in a cute little grey paper bag with the university's logo on it, Maria would love that as a keepsake. I don't know what is in the welcome pack, I figure it's something to look at later, when my eyes don't feel like they have paper cuts, and besides, more and more people are entering the room now, and it's getting a little claustrophobic, and not to mention the fact that I obviously stick out like a sore thumb.

I get through the rest pretty smoothly, just exchanging a brief 'hello' with people, and taking whatever they give me. I must have been given about four or five different brochures already for extracurricular activities by now, where am I even gonna put all of this stuff.

I get to the end and it's a little brown stool sat in front of a camera. Great, can the ground just swallow me up now please?

"What's your name love?" a middle-aged man with grey hair asks me as he ushers me to the stool.

"Mollie Fitzgerald," I say as I take my seat.

"Great Mollie, well this picture is for your student card, this will give you discounts in places and also act as a key to access places like the library."

"Oh, okay, that's cool," I say trying to ignore the fact that everyone else in the room who is waiting is now staring at me.

"I just need you to let your hair down," he says casually.

"Oh, my hair is an absolute mess," I say quietly. "I have just been on an eight-hour flight."

"Sorry, love," he says, campus rules.

What kind of stupid rule is that? I think to myself as I begin to pry a hairband out of my knotty hair. This photo is going to look absolutely awful! Do I really need more of a reason to be embarrassed right now?

But looking at the bigger picture, I just oblige and get it out of the way, my hair puffed out around me all curly like a lion's mane, what a sight to behold and you can bet your life that as soon as the flash went off, I was right there with the band, pulling it up into a bun.

"Here you go," he says, handing me a key card, the worst picture in existence, and I have to carry it with me every day, how lucky am I?

As I walk out of that room towards the exit, I take a look back at everyone waiting in line, all the girls caked in makeup with perfect hair all ready for it, I guess I never got that memo.

Twenty-two

This cinema was amazing, the Odeon I believe it was called, looked completely different to the one I had visited four or five years back. The smell of sweet popcorn filled my body from my very first step inside, TV screens hanging up above us advertising the latest movies, families all around us preparing to enter their own movies, and the biggest pic 'n' mix stand I had ever seen in my life. Trying to play it cool, I just followed Dom's lead to the till. I think I had already made enough of a fool out of myself by dramatically staring at the bread counter the other day, I didn't want him to think that I was a complete lunatic.

Like some kind of professional, Dom got our tickets sorted in under a minute. He even got to choose where we sat! Since when was that a thing? It made sense having allocated seating, but I wondered how many people actually sticked to it?

"Do you want a small or medium popcorn?" Dom asked, as he ordered a medium for himself. The cashier looked at me as if he wanted me to hurry up, but I felt a little uncomfortable still, with people buying things for me.

"Small, please," I said to Dom politely, I knew it was the cheaper option, and they must be paying a fortune for the zoo tomorrow.

Within seconds, the man prepared it and Dom paid. He also grabbed us both a bottle of Fanta each, saying that he remembered I liked it from when we were at Nando's — who knew he had been paying this much attention?

I didn't know whether it was because he saw me drooling at it, or he just wanted it himself, but I found myself standing in front of the sweets with a scoop in one hand, and a bag in the other. I didn't think we needed to do anything tomorrow, I was being spoilt enough today!

Again, not wanting to spend too much, I scooped five or six cola bottles into my bag and a handful of jelly beans, that would do me for sure.

"Are you sure that is all you want?" Dom said, looking at me with a raised eyebrow.

"Yes, please, thank you," I said smiling at him.

"You're the easiest kid in the world," he said as he ruffled my hair. "Most kids would have had one of everything in their bag by now."

"Just as well I'm not like most kids then," I said, trying to flatten my hair back into shape.

"No, you're way cooler," he jokes as we finish paying and walked into screen twelve.

As we walked deeper and deeper into the room, we became engulfed in darkness, a few lights on each wall, illuminating everything, just enough for you to be able to see where you were walking. As we turned to our left, we were standing in front of about two hundred red recliner-style chairs. The popcorn smell was fading with each step, and the scent of an elderly gentlemen's hotdog filled my nose quickly. Maybe I should have got one of those instead? No, they would have cost a fortune.

Following very closely behind Dom, as we walked past rows and rows of seats right to the very back, apparently it was the best place to sit; I'd have to be the judge of that one. As I took my seat, I quickly scanned the rest of the room, I took note of everyone else in here, no one sat anywhere near us, everyone else close to the front; guess they'd never got Dom's memo.

Aside from the elderly gentlemen and his grandson, there were about six other people all spread out, mainly in pairs. Kind of like us. I wondered if anyone else was in the same situation? Probably not.

With *Wreck it Ralph* being a cartoon, it wasn't rocket science that this would be mainly full of children, and as more and more flowed in, as the film got closer to starting, there were barely any seats left.

Sitting next to me was a little girl, probably about four or five, long icy-blonde hair flowing elegantly into her blue dungarees, matched with white tights. By the looks of things, she had come with her mother, who was the spitting image of her daughter. I wonder if I would have been the spitting image of my mother? Or my father even? If he had stuck around.

By the sounds of it, Dom had a freak-show the other side of him. They'd only been sat down five minutes and already we had heard three children crying and a father scolding them aggressively. I was glad I was not them.

"Don't worry," Dom leant over and whispered to me, "They'll shut up when the film starts."

I laughed and before we knew it, the lights had faded to full darkness, and the screen directly in front of us illuminated the title in red letters. I just hoped I didn't fall asleep on these comfy chairs. I scooped the popcorn and sweets into my mouth in turns and sipped the Fanta generously.

The movie was good, it wasn't what I was expecting, it was better. Dom was glued to the screen for the whole duration, he didn't even notice when the kid next to him stole some of his popcorn, bless him.

I knew it was only a movie, but the whole way through, I just kept feeling so sorry for Ralph, like he was destined to be a bad-guy in his game, not by choice, and even after he tried to be nice and mingle with the other people, they were scared of him, and I thought it showed a bigger message of how sometimes, people will do anything to fit in or to achieve something. It's easy to be picked on as the outcast, and not in the same way, but I felt like I could relate to him a little bit.

We decided to wait until the seats were mostly empty before we started to leave. Dom said that there was no point joining a queue full of people pushing and shoving, which I was secretly relived about. Made me wonder though, was that the real reason, or was he just trying to buy some more time? I actually didn't think about Maria the whole time during the movie, and I was a little apprehensive about coming here, because I didn't think I would be able to relax, knowing that she was putting so much effort into something for me. The first time I had fully blocked out everything in my mind in years and all because of *Wreck It Ralph*? Who would have thought?

The cinema felt pretty deserted as we started to head out of the main exit, quite peaceful in a way, and I thought that popcorn was forever going to be my new favourite smell.

I enjoyed spending today with just him, and now I had two movie buddies, albeit Maria's movie days in bed were definitely less expensive. Now all I could do was focus my energy on tomorrow and try and contain the excitement for the last few hours before we all went to bed.

Twenty-three

Connie was right about the building being tall and grey, it towers over absolutely anything in sight, windows stacked on top of each other emphasising the many floors it must have. The door, a brown painted wood covered in cobwebs and spiders, my skin crawls slightly as I walk towards it to push open the door that has been left ajar.

The smell inside here, as I take my first steps, is very musky, maybe even a little damp. The walls are painted the same grey as outside, but they are covered in fingerprints and the odd speck of mud. I'm starting to retract my earlier relief that I wasn't picked for a sorority maybe that would have been better for me.

Directly in front of you as you walk in further is a brown staircase leading about fifteen steps up. There is a door to the left saying kitchen, and one to the right saying bathroom, and that is pretty much it for downstairs, no pictures on the walls, no welcome mat, no pretty chandelier. You can tell why this place wasn't mentioned in their online brochure.

Walking up the stairs, as I have no choice but to at this point, I lug my suitcase up each step, the wheels crashing loudly against the splintering wood underneath my feet, and all I can do is pray that the stairs don't give in.

Thinking back to what Connie said, about me being on the top floor, I am suddenly starting to think maybe I should have eaten beforehand, but here I am, on my eighth or ninth step, and all I can do is power through.

Strangely enough, the top of this floor is exactly the same as downstairs, the same kitchen and toilet doors either side and a staircase leading upwards, just facing the other way. The only difference is a white glass door straight ahead that says, 'First Floor Dorms'. I guess they use words instead of numbers to navigate around here.

Not wanting to stand still and take in everything else, due to tiredness, and the fact that the smell is getting worse with each step, I find strength that I never knew I had, and pull the suitcase quickly and quietly. I'm scared that if I stop, I won't be able to start going again.

I finally get to the top floor, as sweat pours from every part of my body. I contemplated removing my cardigan at one point, but that would just be one extra thing to have to carry, and my hands are red raw with blisters.

Interestingly enough, we have no kitchen or bathroom on our floor by the looks of it. How fantastic, just means that when you need to go you need to travel even further to go to the one a level down from us. Great.

With the same as all the other floors, I see the same white glass door, except this time I walk over to it and push it open. My feet are instantly greeted with a dark green carpet covered in black smudges of god knows what, and the walls are more of a charcoal colour instead of a grey.

It's a corridor right ahead of me, three doors on the left, and two on the right, nothing but a tiny strip of LED lighting to illuminate the way to go. It's a good thing I have always eaten my carrots.

I get to the door 370 and I hesitate deeply as I use my key to open it. Praying that what is waiting inside, the place where I will be spending the rest of my life here, is a lot better, and not as germ ridden. Surely, with us being from overseas, you would have thought they would have put us up somewhere fancy to try and make a good impression? But then again, maybe all the other dorms are like this, and they just used a bit of Photoshop on their pictures.

I push open the door, and am greeted by a welcoming citrus smell, that I recognise all too well to be some kind of disinfectant. The room is bigger than I thought it would be, windows lining the back wall, hardwood flooring, three single beds, all in their own corners, a desk and chair next to each, and a clothes rack in the middle of the room. That must be the wardrobe.

As I pull in my suitcase behind me, I notice instantly the buzzing of the light swaying above my head, just a bulb, no lightshade or anything.

"Excuse me, you can't just barge in to someone else's room." A voice viciously snaps at me as a girl emerges from behind the clothing rack, long ginger hair, a thick Irish accent, and a very tight, red, body-hugging dress that leaves absolutely nothing to the imagination.

"Erm, I live here," I say, trying not to sound as rude as her, but struggling.

"Show me your key," she demands as she steps towards me, black pumps clanking against the floor.

"Fine," I say, as I throw the key in her direction for her to catch, she looks at it, and then at me and throws it back.

"Very well," she says, still rudely. "You have to have that bed," she says pointing to the one next to the door. "Me and Samira are having these, because they are closer together and we are already best friends."

Not even bothering to rise to it, I walk towards my new area and set my case down on the floor "So I'm Mollie," I say, trying to make polite conversation, as I start to unzip my case to unpack. After all, I am going to have to live with her, might as well try and find some common ground. "I'm from England."

"Yeah, that was obvious from your accent, I'm from Ireland if you couldn't work it out, and my name is Heather. My friends call me Hetti, but you can call me Heather." She turns her back to me and walks over to her own bed. She can't have been here long because, the same as me, her case is still on the floor and very much unopened.

"Nice to meet you," I say, avoiding eye contact.

"We weren't aware we would have to share with someone else," she hisses back. "You weren't here for enrolment a few weeks back."

"No," I say, still sounding polite, always got to try and be the bigger person. "I enrolled online through video call, we didn't have the money to be forking out for two trips."

"Oh, brilliant," she says as I can see her in the corner of my eyes, huffing and puffing. "Just what I wanted, come to Washington, and stay with a poor girl."

"Well, we must both be pretty poor if we both have to stay in this dump," I say, as I turn to face her. "We may be foreigners here, but there is nothing a little money can't help you get, so I'll start again. My name is Mollie, I am from England, and I will be staying here with you both, despite the fact I was not present for enrolment, just like half the people here weren't, as they did enrolment over a period of three weeks." I turn away with a smug look on my face. She doesn't reply, instead, she just rolls her eyes at me and continues to wipe her desk with an anti-bacterial wipe. I just can't wait to meet Samira, if she is anything like Heather, I just know this place will be a dream come true, but if anything it is giving me leverage to stay here. The fact I know they don't want me here, just makes it that all more appealing. If they want to try and make my life miserable, I might as well do the same back, after all, it will take my mind off of things for a while.

Because this is going to be one long ride — and I have one hell of a long way to go.

This is not the end of my story — it's just the beginning.